BLOOD OF THE FAE

THE FAE CHRONICLES #2

VALIA LIND

CW01080664

Copyright © 2021 by Valia Lind

All rights reserved.

No part of this book may be reproduced in any form or by any electronic or mechanical means, including information storage and retrieval systems, without written permission from the author, except for the use of brief quotations in a book review.

This is a work of fiction. Names, places, characters and incidents are either the product of the author's imagination or are used fictitiously, and any resemblance to any actual persons, living or dead, organizations, events or locales is entirely coincidental.

Cover by Anika at Ravenborn Designs

BLOOD OF THE FAE

THE FAE CHRONICLES - BOOK TWO

Valia Lind

The world spins round,
The time flies by.
The day has changed,
The time has come.

The war is here,
As the Ancients rise.
One true hero,
Must take up the fight.

The winds are changing,
As the powers grow.
The night is coming,
But the break of dawn—is not far at all.

CHAPTER 1

I've been staring at the mirror for the last ten minutes, willing the wings to appear once more. Nora is busy packing a bag for me while the guys have disappeared to do their own preparation. I should help or something. But I can't stop staring at myself.

Pulling my hair gently over my ear, I study the upward arch and the pointed end. So far, only Derek has seen this new addition. It's probably wise for me to keep it that way. The wings have stirred enough controversy for now. Queen Svetlana is not happy with my display of power. She was trying to keep me a secret, but that went out the window. That's why she's sending me on this pointless mission.

It's for sure pointless. And dangerous. She's playing with me, but that's fae. I have no choice but to go along. I need answers even more than she needs my power, and this is my only chance. Plus, putting some distance between myself and this palace is an added bonus.

"Are you ready?" Nora comes out of my walk-in closet, and I drop my hair back in place quickly. She holds a cross-body bag in one hand and a jacket in the other. I look down at my dress.

"Let me change."

It takes me five minutes to get into my jeans and t-shirt. The moment the clothes are on, I feel more like myself. Not that I don't love the fancy dresses I've been wearing, but they haven't been mine. Since everything else in my life seems to belong to someone else, I need something of mine right now.

When I step out of the closest, Derek and Julian are back. Both of the guys are in dark pants and dark shirts. Julian is already in a jacket while Derek shrugs his on. They turn to look at me, and no matter how hard I try, I can't read either one of them. Right now, they look more fae than I've ever seen them, even though they're dressed in human clothes. I wonder if that's meant to make me feel better or if the clothes make them more comfortable.

"We need to go. The queen has already inquired about our status." Derek speaks in that detached tone of his. I hate when he sounds like that. It reminds me just how little I can trust him.

"It's been less than an hour," I comment.

"She likes to be obeyed immediately," Nora mumbles, handing over a jacket. I put it on before I pull the strap of the bag on as well.

I grab the hair tie around my wrist and pull half of my hair away from my face, keeping it low enough to hide the ears. Derek doesn't miss the move, his eyes steadily on me.

Once I'm done, I face the guys as we eye each other. If anyone asks, I will lie and say I'm ready. But in reality, my insides are a mess, and I feel like I'm going to throw up. I'm more nervous than I can put into words.

"Avery." Nora's voice breaks through my internal freak out. She steps into my line of sight, forcing my eyes on her. "Trust your instincts above all else. The magic of the forest," she lowers her voice, "it's messy and manipulative. But if you trust yourself, you will get through it."

"That's the problem, isn't it?" I chuckle without any humor. I don't trust myself or my magic. When I found that book at Thun-

BLOOD OF THE FAE

derbird Academy and read the words that haven't been read in centuries, everything I knew about magic went up in flames.

Nora places her hand on my shoulders, meeting my eyes.

"You are stronger than you give yourself credit for. Remember that."

The intensity behind her words doesn't escape me. Fae can't lie, and therefore, she truly believes what she says. It's a good reminder. I just need to get to this level.

"Keep us updated when you can," Derek tells Nora as she steps back. She nods and then it's time.

The queen is sending us to the eastern front, or close to it, to fetch one of the ancient fae books no one but me can read. It seems like so much more than just a simple test though. I'm determined to pass whatever obstacle she throws my way. I'm sure this won't be the only one. She expects me to fail, and I refuse to give her the satisfaction. That thought will have to guide me through what comes next.

"We'll portal into the area and go from there," Derek says. I understand what he's not saying. We have our own mission underneath the one the queen has given us. While I don't trust fae as far as I can throw them, right now, I need them.

"Let's do this then."

* * *

THE PORTAL IS a ripple in the air in front of us. I step through it with no hesitation, much like I did at Thunderbird Academy. Derek leads the way with Julian right behind me. I glance back just in time to watch Nora disappear from view.

When I turn back to the guys, their attention is on the forest around us. I hear it right away, the low hum of activity that surrounds us on every side. The forest is restless.

"We're not too far from the eastern front. There's a base camp to the south, About a two-hour walk or so."

"Why so far?" I ask, facing Derek. He pulls his attention from the forest and looks over at me.

"Since the Ancients are on the borders, magic here is very regulated. The queen doesn't want to unnecessarily fuel something they're doing with her magic. I'm sure you've heard about their syphoning powers."

"Yes."

Everyone knows about what happened in Hawthorne two years ago, and at Thunderbird Academy last school year. The Ancients have a way of getting inside even the most protected areas and then infecting the magical creatures with a disease that steals their magic and kills them slowly. This has happened in many places over the last few years, and it's something the witches are constantly working to prevent. I was going to be on the council to help fight this problem...before my life changed entirely.

"The fae are weaker than anyone would like to admit," Julian says, coming to stand beside me. "We have to take every precaution."

It's one of the few times he's put himself in the same category as the fae, and I take notice. These boys might be different than most of the fae, but they're still here for themselves and their homeland. I can't forget that.

"So, what do we do?"

"We go the other direction."

Derek turns north, squaring his shoulders. He's worried, I think. I can't read his emotions as easily as I could at the cabin. But I do think we're still connected on some level. Despite all the secrets he's keeping, he's been helping me. Or something along those lines. There's tension in his shoulders and determination on his face.

"Anyone going to tell me exactly what awaits us in the forbidden forest?" I ask as we start walking. The trees here are so much bigger than I've ever seen before. At first, I think my eyes are deceiving me. But as I blink a few times, I realize there's a shine around every piece of nature, including individual leaves and blades of grass. Pausing, I reach over to run my fingertips over the closest branch, completely in awe. The magic is in every living thing here. It almost calls to me. It's so beautiful, I think I could stay here forever.

"Avery?" Suddenly, Derek is in front of me, leaning down to catch my eye.

"What?"

"Are you okay? You've been standing frozen for a few minutes."

"I—" I turn back to the leaf, my fingers still touching it gently. Maybe it doesn't *almost* call to me, maybe it *actually* does. And that's dangerous. I remember what Nora said about the pull of the forest. I'll have to be more proactive about keeping myself protected.

"I feel it, Derek," I say, glancing up at him. "I feel the magic in the air and in the leaves and in the ground beneath my feet. It's like... I don't know how to explain it."

But I do. I just don't want to say it out loud. It feels like I belong here, and I have no idea what to do with that.

"Faery is filled with magic, Avery," Derek says, reaching over and tugging gently on the front of my jacket. I step away from the branches, dropping my arm. "There is a lot of it in you. Magic you don't yet understand."

He pauses, as if he's trying to figure out what else to say, but I shrug it off.

"Yes. Let's get going. I'll keep up."

An emotion flashes in Derek's eyes, too quick for me to decipher. He nods and turns away, dropping the front of my jacket back into place. I meet Julian's eye as Derek moves past him. There's something there too, but these fae are good at keeping their emotions under lock and key. I need to take some pointers.

Without a word, I follow Derek as Julian brings up the rear.

CHAPTER 2

he forest grows darker and fuller around us as we walk. The buzz of magic I felt in the air from the beginning has only intensified. There's a film of static over my skin, and I'm hyperaware of every move we make.

Having fae magic is a new experience, one I don't know what to do with yet. I keep expecting the wings to burst out of my back, but of course, that's just dumb. Or maybe it's not. I have no idea. Not knowing things is very frustrating and not at all pleasant.

"So, how do we know when we've reached the forbidden forest?" I break the silence while still keeping my voice low. I'm smart enough to know there are things hiding in the trees that might not want us here. We have to be careful, but at the same time, I need at least small amounts of information to stay sane.

"We'll know," Derek replies without turning around or slowing down. I roll my eyes at him, even though he can't see it, and I hear Julian chuckle. Glancing over my shoulder, I notice him shake his head before he looks over at me.

"What?"

"Nothing."

I narrow my eyes but don't push further. The intuitive part of me thinks I don't want to know what's going on in Julian's head anyway.

We walk for a few more moments in silence before Julian appears at my side, keeping pace. I wait for him to speak, since he clearly wants to say something. After a few minutes, he finally does.

"The forbidden forest carries magic within in, just like the rest of Faery. The difference is that it's almost dense in a way. The moment we pass the border, it'll feel like we're carrying a physical weight."

I narrow my eyes, mulling over the information. Faery is one of those places that, no matter how much I study about it, I still know next to nothing. I am severely unprepared for the direction my life has turned.

"Is this a well-known fact, or have you been here before?"

"I haven't."

Julian doesn't have to add anything else because I hear the end of that sentence. Derek has. I shift my eyes toward the prince, who's a little way ahead of us now. Once again, I wonder about him. I really should stop, but I'm not going to. It's foolish to pretend I'm not curious about him.

We fall back into silence, the only noise coming from the forest around us. I keep expecting something bad to happen or some attack to come at us from beyond the shadows, but there's nothing. It's almost as if the world around me is also holding its breath, curious to see what will happen next.

The tips of my ears tingle just then, and I reach for them before I can stop myself. It's not an unpleasant feeling, but it's also a very strange sensation. My hair still covers the tips, but when I run my fingers over it, the pointed end is there.

"What is it?" Julian asks, coming up beside me. He fell back behind me, but now he's watching me curiously. He hasn't seen my ears yet, and I drop my hand quickly before replying.

"I'm not sure."

"Avery, are you sensing something?" Derek asks, backtracking to stand in front of me. I send a glare his way because Julian is now ready to ask all the questions.

"What's going on?"

Resigned, I tuck my hair behind my ear as I say, "The wings weren't the only thing to show up with my magic."

When Julian's eyes land on my ear, he takes an automatic step back. Derek does a double take as well, and my heartbeat speeds up at their alarm.

"What?"

Neither one speaks, so I raise my hand and snap my fingers in front of their face. They visibly jerk, as if coming out of a trance, turning their gazes on me.

"You guys need to learn how to voice your concerns. What's happening?"

Julian clears his throat, but it's Derek who finally replies.

"May I?" His hand reaches for my hair, and I have no choice but to nod. He pulls it away from my ear, studying it like he's never seen anything like it before. I try not to fidget under the scrutiny, but both of them are making it very difficult.

"Derek?" I finally prob when his fingers brush gently over the tip of the ear, sending a flood of goosebumps down my arm.

"It's something I haven't seen before."

"What, an earlobe?"

"No," Derek steps back, letting my hair fall back against my scalp. He stays close enough that I have to look up to meet his gaze. "Your skin, it has been…painted."

"What?" Look at that, it's my favorite word.

"There's a sort of design, almost like your veins are full of gold that wraps itself around your ear." He says it gently, but panic comes anyway. My hand flies up to my ear. I rub it and move it around, but I can't feel anything.

"I need to see."

"We're not exactly carrying a mirror with us."

I step over to Derek, push his jacket aside, and yank the bl. from the sheath around his waist. He doesn't even react to my proximity as I raise the blade with my right hand and move my hair to see better. It's distorted, but even I can see the golden lines wrapping themselves around my skin. I move to the other side, looking at my right ear, but there's nothing there.

"It's only on my left?"

"It appears so."

"What does it mean?"

I glance from Derek to Julian to Derek again, but they have no answers for me. It's evident that they haven't seen this before, which raises my concern. I can't even demand answers because they don't have any.

My body continues to change in strange ways, and there's nothing anyone can do about it. Not even me.

It's another few hours of walking before Derek decides it's time to stop for the night. We find a small clearing. While Julian is tasked with putting together a fire, Derek disappears into the trees to make sure we're truly alone.

He hasn't said a word to me since the golden design appeared on my ear. He seems to be more concerned than I am. I guess maybe a part of me is getting used to the fact that nothing about me is what I thought.

All my life I just thought I was the normal kind of weird. Half witch, half shifter. Not exactly accepted by the standard magical community, but the blunder my parents created by falling in love is more known than not. Adding to the fact that I have fae blood in me somehow? That's a blunder no one will ever forgive. Maybe not even me.

My parents lied to me. Of that I am sure. The only logical explanation I can come up with is they were waiting to tell me the truth. Maybe once I became a Watcher and would be more protected by the council because of my standing with them, then my parents would be able to be honest with me. Or maybe they were going to keep this from me forever.

The logical side of my brain is working to understand their situation. The emotional side is just hurt they kept such a huge secret from me.

Mad.

Frustrated.

Betrayed.

"Are you okay?" Julian asks, looking up as the fire begins to crackle. The flames dance across Julian's face, and he's not hiding his concern as he studies me.

"I'm working on it," I reply, taking a seat as I shake away the feelings and grab a stick to poke at the fire. It gives me something to do, and Julian doesn't question it. Instead, he takes a seat opposite of me, lapsing into silence.

I have so many things I want to ask him. I've learned a little bit about him since he appeared at the palace, but both he and Derek confuse me so much. I see the way Queen Svetlana is. I watched how the others behave within the palace walls. But these two fae seem nothing like that, and I can't wrap my mind around it.

"So that whole stealing from the Council plan you had back in Arizona, was that just part of the ruse?" I ask Julian, as I tend to the fire. My question clearly takes him by surprise, and he watches me for a second before he replies.

"No." He's silent for a moment, as if he's contemplating how much to tell me. "It was really going to be a way for me to get away. My mission...I didn't have a choice to come find you. But I might've gotten away if we went through with it."

I can't blame him for wanting more out of life than to follow someone else's rules. I guess none of us really have a choice in all of this. But I never thought he wouldn't. I'm learning more and more about the way of the fae, and I have to admit, they're not my favorite people. Or creatures. Or whatever the proper term is because I'm not even sure about that anymore. A lot of good all my education is doing for me now. But I can't really blame the education, just the people who wouldn't teach me what I actually needed to know.

Yes, I'm back to being mad at my parents. Apparently, this will come in waves.

"Why are you and Derek so different from the other fae?" I risk the question, turning my attention to the present. I reach for my bag and pull out some fruit as I wait for Julian to answer. He seems to need a moment to collect his thoughts. When he finally replies, his words are barely a whisper.

"Because we want more for ourselves."

Pausing, I glance over at Julian, but his eyes are on the fire. He seems a hundred miles away. His expression is unguarded, and I realize, it's maybe for the first time since I've met him. There's history there. If Derek was sitting next to him right now, I wonder if his face would carry the same look of wanderlust. But maybe I don't have to wonder. I've seen the way he is with the queen. Regardless of his betrayal toward me, the need for things to be different is real. If nothing else, I can trust that.

"Do you really think I can make that happen?" I ask because I need to know this isn't all in vain. The fear that I'll make things worse is ever present. But before Julian has a chance to reply, another voice speaks up from the shadows.

"We know you will."

Derek steps into the circle of the light, his eyes reflecting the dance of the flames. There's that intensity again, the Derek I'm used to seeing. He truly believes what he's saying, and at this moment, I have no choice but to trust him. Trust both of them. Everyone has something at stake here.

CHAPTER 3

a sudden blast of magic jerks me awake. I sit up, panting, as I glance around to see where it came from. But the night is completely quiet. Julian is asleep a few feet to my left on the other side of the fire. The closer we've gotten to the forbidden forest, the less noise the trees around us make. Right now, it's especially unnerving.

I search for Derek and find him a dozen feet away, barely outlined against the tree he's leaning against. His gaze is on me. I don't have to see it to know it's true. My skin prickles with awareness.

Since coming to Faery and finding out the truth about Derek's lineage, we've been in this constant state of suspension. I think if we were still at the cabin, he would come to me. Or maybe I'd go to him. But now, neither one of us knows how to act around the other.

This trip is at least giving us a chance to do something. Whatever it may be. I don't trust Queen Svetlana, but I'm also having a difficult time trusting myself. I hold powers I didn't even know existed. And the land around me is reacting to it.

How I wish for the comfort of books right now. I want my

notebooks and big research encyclopedia volumes filled with information. I want a large table where I can sit for hours and pour over the history of Faery and the Ancients. But I don't have any of that. All I have is the memory of a book that I should've never read and the weight of worlds on my shoulders.

I'm not so naive that I don't know what would happen if Faery falls. It would spill into other worlds, other dimensions. There would be no rest for anyone because the Ancients would win.

And they are not kind rulers.

Since waking up, their stories have finally been told, after generations of keeping them secret. I've done all the research I could to learn about them and how they operate, and it's not enough. They want me, and that's a constant fear I carry in my heart.

The same feeling that woke me up returns, magic shaking me from inside. Looking down, I watch as my palm ignites with fire. It's the elemental magic I've carried with me since birth. It's been giving me problems for months now, even before I started at Thunderbird Academy.

But it hasn't acted on its own before.

It makes me feel like I'm a little kid again, just coming into my powers. I've been told my whole life that magic is fueled by emotions, and right now, I have no idea what's going on inside of me.

Just as quickly as the flame ignites, it's extinguished. Only it's not extinguished by my will but by another form of elemental magic. Water pools in my palm. It douses the fire, which dissipates without a sound.

This water magic is a new development and not something I thought was possible. Most elemental witches carry one element within them, while they can respond to others. But to have control over more than one? It's rare and terrifying.

The buzz of magic rushes over my skin as the water spills over onto the ground, as if I've just poured a cup. It's like the land itself

VALIA LIND

is responding to my magic. Leaning down, I watch the water disappear. My palm ignites in fire again, this time, against the dirt. Then, the space around me glows, and I feel my newest additions before I see them.

"Wow."

Turning, I notice Julian sit up. His eyes are on me. Derek has moved closer as well, and they're both staring. I glance over my shoulder. The glow from my wings is the most beautiful light I've ever seen.

The wings are clear with a bluish outline and so shiny, they're blinding. For a moment, I sit mesmerized, but then they move. My heart thuds harshly, as if I've just come through a jump scare, but I don't dare breathe too loudly. The desire to touch them is overwhelming. The moment the thought comes into my head, they move again. This time they open completely, so they're within easy reach.

I raise my left hand, swinging it backwards under the wings before I let my fingers walk over the edges. The sensation is almost indescribable. It's similar to how it felt having Derek touch the tip of my fae ear.

Intimate.

Tingly.

Breathtaking.

Glancing over my right shoulder, I do the same thing, letting my fingers explore. Even though I possess magic and can wield fire, and now water, this still feels surreal somehow. Like it's not me who's experiencing this phenomenon.

Derek and Julian have both moved closer, but they don't reach for my wings.

"I've never seen something so beautiful," Julian whispers. I look over to find him completely mesmerized. He looked surprised by my ears, but he looks in awe at my wings. When my eyes find Derek's, he looks just as amazed as Julian. But his eyes aren't on

14

the wings, they're on me. It's difficult not to let the hundreds of emotions rush into me right then and there.

Wanting.

Needing.

Begging.

"Are there no fae that have wings?" I dare to ask, even though I know it'll break the atmosphere. But I can't let myself be ruled by hormones, or whatever this is. I have to stay on track.

"No," Julian replies. I'm still watching Derek, so I see the moment his jaw twitches.

"Derek?" I prompt.

"There were stories," he replies with a sigh, "of old families with the power of the wings. It used to be common for fae, but it's a magic that has long ago gone dormant."

"Not so dormant, I suppose," I say, reaching for my wings once again. But before I can touch them, they're gone. As if they were never there.

"I don't understand. Where do they go?"

"Back inside of you."

That doesn't answer anything, but when I open my mouth to ask more, Derek turns away.

"We should get some rest," he throws over his shoulder as he stomps away. Okay, maybe stomps is too dramatic, but it feels like he's being dramatic right now. I roll my eyes but don't argue.

However, instead of laying on my back, I turn to my side. Even though they're no longer there, I fear I might squish them. And they're too beautiful for that.

I SLEEP, but I don't rest. When it's time to move, we have a quick breakfast from the fruit Nora packed for us, and then we're off. Each of us is silent, lost in our own little world. I keep going over what happened last night, the way my magic reacted to the land. And then the wings.

A lost magic. And I have it.

If I'm being honest with myself, I have more than one, and that's scary. I'm trying really hard not to the think about the whole book magic right now because I can only handle so much at a time. So, the wings are where I focus. There is something that's not sitting right with me after last night.

I hurry to catch up with Derek because he's the only one who can provide any kind of answers right now. He's ignoring me extra hard this morning, but I'm relentless.

"What did you mean last night about the families?" I ask, diving right into it. He glances over at me, and I swear there's a spark of amusement in his eyes before he snuffs it out.

"Just like that?"

"Yes, just like that. No reason to beat around the bush." He crunches his eyebrows down in confusion, but I press on. "You have information. I need information. Share. It's that simple."

"Nothing about us is simple, Avery."

The way he says my name sends a plethora of tingles down my back, but I try not to show it. I should not be reacting like this to anything Derek does. Especially the sound of my name on his lips. Yet, my traitorous body has other ideas. It gets all warm and bubbly around him.

What am I even thinking right now? Focus, Avery.

Somehow, I'm afraid Derek can tell what's going on in my mind. So, I put on my best glare and don't let up.

"That may be true, *Derek*, but it doesn't change the fact that you know something. Tell me."

"You're bossy today."

"As opposed to other days? Don't change the subject."

I don't turn around, but I swear I hear Julian chuckle behind us. He's wisely staying out of this. I think Derek is about to argue some more, but then he surprises me.

"There's not much I can tell you, to be honest. The old families, they're not exactly welcomed at court."

"Why is that?"

"Because Queen Svetlana does not like to be one upped in her own palace."

The purely human phrase stumps me for a moment because, even though he usually sounds human, he still surprises me when he says something like that. Then, I realize the other thing I've noticed. He never refers to Queen Svetlana as his mother. Maybe that distance can work in my favor.

"So, who were they? Just other fae who lived in court?"

"From what I understand, the families were all part of a ruling council. Yes, the king sat on the throne, but the council was there to advise and protect. They had the most powerful of Faery magic, and they protected and nourished the land with it."

"Because fae are so connected to the land." It's not a question, but Derek replies anyway.

"Fae need nature, but nature needs the fae. It's a balance of give and take, and it's the most powerful when it's balanced. When Queen Svetlana took the throne, she didn't want balance. She wanted power. So, killing off the council was in her best interest."

"She's that old?" I ask, before I stop to think about it. This time Julian definitely chuckles. Derek manages to mask most of his smile.

"You forget fae live for a long time, Avery." He looks down at me at those words, and there's almost a hint of sadness there. "She is older than she appears, one of the oldest in the land. There's a reason she's held power for this long."

That means she is ruthless, and here we are, disobeying her orders. I'm not sure how I feel about any of this, but I don't have time to mull over it because we're no longer alone.

The feeling comes at once, as if a door has been opened, and we can see beyond it. I'm instantly on alert. A moment later, so are

Derek and Julian. I wonder why I sensed it before they did, but I'm not about to question it.

"Avery, you'll need your magic," Derek mumbles as he reaches for his sword. Julian is beside us in a flash, his sword already drawn. We don't stop moving. In the next moment, it feels like a heavy weight has been placed on my shoulders. I glance over at the boys, and I know they feel it too.

We have entered the forbidden forest. And we have company.

CHAPTER 4

*E*verything is darker here, but somehow, more vivid. It's like the colors aren't bleached out by being in the sun. We move together, keeping our steps sure. I'd be lying if I said I'm not scared. Whatever is out there, it's hunting us now. It was hunting us before we even entered the borders of the forest.

"We need to find high ground or open space," Derek states without missing a beat. Even without giving our surroundings a thorough study, I know that's not possible. We can climb a tree, but I'm not sure that'll do us any good, since we're being watched.

That's the one thing I know for sure. It's like I can feel the extra pressure of their eyes on me. It adds to the heaviness of the forests. After not resting last night, I wonder how I'm going to fight. Because we'll have to. I can feel it coming.

"Derek, on your left."

"I see it."

I shift my eyes in that direction, but I don't see anything. I don't know what I'm looking for, so I can't even pretend to find it at this point. With Derek in front of me and Julian behind me, I'm between two powerful and trained fae. I should feel better, but I can't shake the feeling that whatever is out there doesn't care about them. It's here for me.

Suddenly, a noise like a thousand wolves hounding fills the air, nearly overpowering my eardrums. Grabbing my ears, I look around, trying to figure out where it's coming from. Before we get our bearings, another noise reaches us. Happy yapping scatters all around us.

I glance up. It takes me a second to realize what I'm seeing.

"Are those..." I shout to be heard over the noise.

"Boggarts." Derek and Julian shout together.

I've only ever read about the creatures in books. They don't hang out in the forests around my hometown. They're nasty creatures. Their huge eyes are the size of saucers, and they have lanky limbs. The creatures are about the size of a calf, their skin leather-like. Their arms are so long, they almost reach to the ground. The hair that covers their whole bodies is shaggy and dirty. I can smell them even from a few dozen feet away.

The noise they make is disorienting, their first line of offense. Some can leap up to ten feet in the air and forward, which makes getting away nearly impossible. From what I read, there are dozens of types of these creatures, but none of them are ever nice in the stories. They look like they can rip us limb from limb.

"We need to move. They smelled us even before we stepped into the forbidden part of the forest." It's hard to hear Derek over the noise, but I get the gist of it. The boggarts were lying in wait. Without a moment to spare, we take off running. The boggarts are on our heels.

They're like a swarm of bees, moving together in a swirl of noise. When the first one lands between us, it throws us in opposite directions. I scream. Yanking the knife I carry on my thigh out of the sheathe, I roll to the left as another creature lands in that spot. I'm on my knees in the next moment, grounding myself as I reach for my fire magic.

The creature leans forward, screaming that awful sound into

my face. I push my pain away as I swipe at it, swinging, somewhat blindly. My blade connects with his skin, and the creature screams in agony. I don't hesitate to blast a line of fire at it, sending it flying a dozen yards back.

My magic ignites, a rush of power over my whole body as I blast another creature away. It seems the more I use it, the happier my magic is. Maybe it's a strange thought, but I don't push it away. I embrace it.

Another creature reaches me. I swipe at it a few times without landing any blows. Then, suddenly, I'm on the ground as another boggart jumps on my back. The thing is strong, clawing at me with its long arms and even longer nails. Even after all the years of battle training, I am not prepared for this. It takes all my strength to stay upright as I try to shake it off while preventing the other from getting to me.

We drop to the ground. I go to roll out of the way, but now two of them are on top of me, tearing at my hair and my skin. My fire magic ignites, sending a blast all around me. The creatures yelp but don't let up. Their leathery skin is protecting them some-how, and the momentum of the fire is diminished by my position. I have to be smarter.

I kick out, managing to land a blow while I swing my arm out again, still holding onto the knife. I need a protection spell, but my mind is so scrambled, I can't focus long enough to call on my power. In the midst of the battle, I'm useless. The thought almost drags me down faster than the boggart grabbing my leg and pulling me toward him. I end up flat on my back once more, throwing my arms up to protect my face as the creatures descend and scream at me.

My body shakes from the sound, disorienting me once more. That's when I stop thinking.

Instincts take over. The next thing I know, a wall of water rushes up out of the ground, sweeping the monsters away. They scream, this time in agony, as the water slams them against the trees and the ground. It takes me a second to realize what happened, but then I jump to my feet. Julian and Derek are to my left. Both of them are now in the protection of my water circle.

"I thought you were a fire elemental," Julian comments, his face a mixture of confusion and awe. He must not have seen my magic flair up last night before the wings appeared.

"Up until a few months ago, I was." Derek doesn't comment, but he looks a bit proud of me. Or maybe I'm making that up.

"We have to move. We don't know how long the water will keep them at bay," he says. Julian and I move immediately. I have no idea how the water knows what I intend for it to do, but it stays up like a wall as we run farther into the forest.

Magic has always been led by emotion, but now, it's like I have an extra layer of connection between me and it. This is something I'll have to ponder when I have more time. All three of us look like we've been through the ringer, but we have no major injuries as far as I can tell.

It's a few minutes before I feel the magic drop off somewhere behind me. I'm not sure how I can feel it, but I know the water has receded.

"They'll be on us soon," I manage to say as we run. "The magic didn't stay up."

Derek doesn't answer right away as we weave in and out of the trees. Between the fighting and the fact that the forest adds an extra layer of exhaustion to our bones, I'm surprised we're moving this fast. But just when I think we might have a shot at this, something changes.

The air in front of us shimmers like a ripple in the air, coming straight down from the sky. There's no time for us to slow down or change direction.

"Derek, what's happening?" I shout just as the anomaly swallows us whole.

* * *

I EXPECT TO FALL THROUGH, but I'm still standing when the lights dissipate. Spinning around, my eyes zero in on Derek and Julian. I breathe a sigh of relief. At least I'm not alone.

When I finally focus on our surroundings, whatever question I had on my lips dies.

We're still in the forest. I think. But everything is different.

The trees surround us just like they did before, except now, they look almost—rotten. Taking a step forward, I reach out to touch the bark, but my hand is snatched back. I look up to find Derek right beside me, his hand on my wrist.

"I wouldn't."

He watches me steadily. The hint of his fingers tingles on my skin, and something passes between us. It feels almost like the comradeship we developed back at the cabin. But then, he drops my hand, and it's gone.

"What is this place?"

Julian comes to stand beside Derek as I ask, and the two exchange a glance. I expect one of them to speak up, but they don't. This whole secrets-keeping shtick they have going on has got to stop. Exhausted, in more ways than one, I place my hands on my hips as I stare them down.

"Both of you need to learn how to speak up. Because if I have to continuously deal with these side glances, I'm going to start throwing punches." There's just enough annoyance in my voice to make it tougher than it usually sounds. I try not to grin. "Well?"

"It's not that we don't want to tell you," Julian begins, as Derek makes the most un-fae snort I've ever heard. Julian and I both stare at him as if he's lost his mind. "Fine, apparently we don't want to tell you," Julian continues. "But having too much information, especially when we have no idea how your magic will react to any of it, is kind of dangerous."

"Good point, but there has to be a way around that. I'm not walking around this... wasteland blindly."

I can smell it now, the potent stink of rotting ground and trees and well, everything. It fills the air with heaviness unlike anything I've ever felt before. If I'm right, I think even the leaves on these trees are spoiled.

"Wasteland is a pretty accurate description," Derek says over his shoulder as he moves forward. Julian and I don't hesitate to follow, even though I'm more than annoyed with him now. Secrets get people killed. I've read enough of our history to know that. I need information.

"Okay cool. Now tell me, where are we?"

"The forbidden forest."

"Is it forbidden because it stinks?" I can't help but ask as we push past some bushes that I try very hard not to touch.

Derek ignores my question, of course.

"It doesn't matter where we are as much as when."

"Wait, what?" I freeze in my tracks, eyebrows raised. Derek and Julian do their whole side glance as I roll my eyes.

"Don't freak out," Julian begins, which makes me a little madder at him than I was a few seconds ago. "Don't let your magic react in any way."

"Stop talking to me like I'm a child, and tell me what's going on!"

"The forbidden forest is full of time loops," Derek says, waving a hand in Julian's direction, as if telling him to stand down.

"Time loops?"

"Yes. The concept is the same as a regular portal, except the destination is another time."

"So what time is this?" I wave my hand around the dying forest.

"A time when the Ancients win."

Whatever snide remark I may have had dies on my lips. I stare at the trees in front of us, cracked and weathered by a storm I haven't yet seen. The sap pours through the cracks, as if the tree itself is crying.

"Does that mean we lose?" I barely get the question past my

lips, as the tightness in my chest intensifies. Derek is in front of me in a flash, looking down into my face.

"No, this is just one possibility. There is no future that is set in stone. Every decision changes the outcome."

I look up at him, pushing air into my lungs. I hate to admit it, but his presence is calming. It's been this way since the moment we went into hiding together. No matter how much I wish that wasn't the case.

"What choices lead us here?"

"That's the tricky part. We don't know. And we don't have a way to get out of here unless we find another one of the time loops."

"So, we're stuck here?" I manage to keep my voice from rising. The magic inside of me is twisting every which way, asking if there's a way it can help. But I can't exactly let it free when I have no idea what it actually does anymore.

"Only for a short time," Julian says. But my eyes are still on the fae in front of me. There's emotion in his eyes once more, a reassurance he's trying to show by letting his guard down. I can't look away. I feel his presence in every cell of my body. I feel calm.

"We should get moving though. We don't know what waits in these shadows," Derek finally says. All I can do is nod.

CHAPTER 5

*W*e've been walking for a while when the forest falls away, and suddenly, we find ourselves staring at an open landscape in front of us. It's burning.

The heavy smell in the air comes from the fires that fill the space before our eyes. The forest should keep going, that much I can tell. But it's been cut down by the awfulness of the flames. The sight breaks my heart.

Derek and Julian stand on each side of me. When I glance at them, I see shock and pain on their faces. This is their home in ruins. It's a future that's a clear possibility.

The flames cast colors and shadows across the scorched ground. Seeing no other way around, Derek gives Julian and I a nod, and we step forward. If anyone looks over and see us, we probably look like three avenging angels, walking through the hellfire. The guys stay on constant alert, their eyes darting in every direction. I'm having a difficult time concentrating on anything as I feel a sadness inside of me. It's more overwhelming than ever before.

With each step, it seems to weigh heavier on me. When tears come, I have no power to stop them.

Derek notices right away. In the blink of an eye, he's in front of me, reaching for my upper arms.

"Avery, what is it? What's wrong?"

"I don't know." I hiccup over my words, trying to blink the tears away. As I raise my head, I feel the tips of my ears tingle, then a flash of bright light surrounds us before it's gone again.

"Avery, your wings. It's your magic—" Julian stops abruptly. I feel it. It's not me crying, it's the earth beneath my feet. When my knees give out, Derek is there to catch me.

"She's so sad," I mumble, leaning against Derek as he wraps his arms around me to keep me against his chest. "Can you feel it? She's crying and burning, a thousand degrees of agony."

The space around us lights up once more as my wings shimmer in and out of sight. I can't stop the tears that pour out of me long enough to fight the magic or the pain. It's like my body isn't my own anymore.

"Derek, we have to move." I hear the urgency in Julian's voice, but it seems so far away, as if he's in another world and I'm still stuck here.

"Derek, now! We have to move!"

The urgency in Julian's words seems to reach through the fog. I raise my head just as Derek pulls me up beside him. That's when I hear it. The stomping of feet. Turning my head, I glance behind us, and I see them.

Trolls. Or what used to pass for trolls.

Derek half carries, half drags me along as we try to put more distance between us and them. There are many creatures that I've only ever read about, but these seem like they went through a mutation. With the way the land is around us, maybe I shouldn't be that surprised.

Both boggarts and trolls hunt in packs, and they seem to thrive in this forest.

The movement and the danger at our backs seems to have shaken me from whatever emotional stupor I've fallen into, and I

27

find my footing once more. Derek glances at me as I begin keeping pace with him, flashing me a quick smile.

"They're too fast!" I shout as I risk another glance behind. The worst of it is that we have nowhere to hide. The space in front of us is wide open and mostly on fire. We'll have to go through it to get to the other side. And we have no idea what's waiting out there.

"We need to..." Derek begins, but whatever he was going to say is lost on me as something drops down on my back. It brings me to the ground.

"Avery!"

I hear the shouts, but I'm too focused on the weight on top of me. Twisting, I try to throw it off, and realize, it's one of the trolls. He must've taken a running start and then leaped. He's only about half my size but heavy. It's like he's filled with rocks.

"Get off!" I shout, trying to drag him off me. He won't budge. He scratches at me, and I raise my arms to block him as I try to push him away. It's the weight of him that keeps him solidly planted on top of me, no matter how much I try to wiggle free.

Then, Derek is there, and the troll flies off, landing a few feet away. He's completely enraged as he shouts, spit flying all around him. Derek drags me to my feet once more, and then, we can't run. The trolls are everywhere.

"Here." Derek thrusts a sword into my hands, and I grab it automatically. Here's to hoping the few lessons I've had are enough. Derek is at my back, and so is Julian. We create a small circle as the trolls surround us. Derek tries talking to them, speaking a language I don't understand. It causes them all to scream louder.

"Aim for their feet. Their skin is too thick to cut through easily." Derek shouts to be heard over the noise. "Cut at the ankles or over the toes. It'll slow them down."

There isn't much more to say after that, and even though I

have questions, I can't ask them. The trolls jump at us, and all I can do is swing my sword.

For creatures who are stocky and heavy, they seem to be very agile. My movements, and that of the guys, carry us apart as I try to do what Derek said. But it's not easy.

Between the screaming the trolls emit, and the smell all around me, I feel disoriented. And I'm weaker than I've been in a while. The fit of tears and pain I went through hasn't left, it's just diminished. All of this is too much. It's like my every sense is being bombarded.

I swing my sword again, this time connecting with one of the trolls. The scream that leaves his large mouth almost sends me on my back. Instead, I push through and swing again, catching another creature.

But the trolls keep coming. Their large teeth snap close to my skin, as if they want to take a piece of me, which actually makes sense if they're rabid. They do seem to be rabid.

Just then, I hear a yell. I turn to see Julian get taken down by three of trolls. They pin down his arm as one takes a big bite out it. The scream shatters through every emotion I'm experiencing and then my magic is there.

My feet propel me toward Julian. At the same moment, I feel a rush of power. When I swing my sword at the creatures, it's fueled by magic. I manage to get all three of them off before Derek reaches us. We pull Julian to his feet as his arm drips with blood.

The trolls seem to be multiplying. There's no way we're getting out of here. We need one of those ripples to show up and take us back to our time. But then Derek does something that surprises me.

"Hold onto him," he says, pushing Julian toward me. I have just enough time to grab him around the waist. There's not much distance between us and the trolls now. It seems that no matter how many we cut down, three take the place of one. Derek motions me back. I drag Julian with me as I watch Derek take a deep breath.

Then, the fae kneels down, thrusting his hands into the dying earth. I can't see his face, but somehow, I think his eyes are closed. There's a moment of silence, as if the whole world is holding her breath to see what he'll do. And then, there's a roar.

The dirt seems to rise like a wave in front of Derek, rushing up and up and up. He doesn't move; he doesn't speak, and then, the earth falls. The wave of dirt rolls, pushing forward, and I can't see the trolls anymore. All I see is descending dirt.

Derek stands. Without a backward look, he rushes toward us, grabbing Julian from me. I stare at the fae in awe, but now is not the time for questions. He pulls Julian away, and I rush after him.

When I glance behind us, I see nothing but piles of dirt.

* * *

WE MOVE AS QUICKLY as we can with Derek half carrying Julian. The heaviness of the land is pressing on my heart. The strong emotions I experienced earlier are threatening to rise up again. It takes everything in me not to stop, not to slow down. All I want to do is lay down in the midst of this dirt and weep.

For the loss of the land's magic. For the loss of her beauty.

My beautiful Faery.

My beautiful Faery.

My beautiful Faery.

"Avery!"

I glance up at Derek's tone and the twinge of panic in it.

"What is it?"

"You went somewhere again. We have to keep going."

I didn't even realize we stopped. These random spacing out episodes...I have no explanation for them. I wish there was a way I could control them, especially right now. Derek waits for me to explain, but I just nod and rush off after him.

"Those were unlike any trolls I've ever seen."

"Just like the boggarts," Julian comments. He's covered in sweat, his arm bleeding again. He's still moving as he leans on Derek, but this position compromises us. If we get attacked right now, I'd have to fight them off, and I have no idea if I'm capable.

"What do you mean?"

"There's something wrong with them. That species isn't how they used to be."

The Ancients. That's got to be it. They're messing with the natural order of things, and that includes the creatures that live in these forests.

I'm on a rollercoaster of emotion and magical discovery. No one should be near me right now, especially those in a life or death situation. Taking a deep breath, I try to stay focused. If I let my mind wander, then I'll start feeling everything. If that happens, we're in trouble. Well, more trouble than we've been.

"Do you have any idea where we are?" I ask as I study our surroundings, looking for the next attack. The sight of the trees rotting from the inside out breaks my heart. There are no leaves on them, the branches are bare and fragile.

"None of this looks familiar."

I was hoping that wasn't the case. Wherever the time jumping ripple dropped us, it's not familiar to either fae to be of much use. We're walking around blindly.

"Maybe I can try something," I say, the idea popping into my mind out of nowhere. Derek stops, depositing Julian carefully to the ground. Both of the fae look at me in question, waiting for me to go on.

"Don't ask what made me think of it, but can I feel the ground? And maybe search for something within it? I feel connected to her." A tear slips down my cheek, and I wipe it away quickly. "Maybe I can find something."

"Using your magic could—"

"You just used your magic," I interrupt, because Derek is probably about to deliver another speech on my unstable magical abilities. I still have questions about him being able to use magic, but now is not the time.

"It's not the same."

"No, it's not. I didn't even know you could do that. But something is telling me I can do this, so you know what, I'm not asking for your permission."

I drop down to my knees immediately, thrusting my hands into the ground. Derek is there in a flash, reaching for me. I bat his hand away.

"It's too dangerous."

"You have to stop trying to protect me from everything." I look him dead in the eye. "I can't keep walking around on eggshells, waiting for my magic to do something else I've never seen before. This way, at least I'm trying to learn to control it. You have to trust me to take care of myself."

There is a lot of emotion behind my words, and if asked, I'll blame it on my connection to this broken land. But if I'm honest with myself, right here and right now, I need Derek to believe in me.

He stares into my eyes for a long moment before finally nodding his head.

"I'll be right here."

He moves only a fraction of a foot away, staying on the ground near me. I glance over at Julian, who's watching me steadily, and then, I let my magic dive.

It pours from inside my being into my hands and then into the ground. I close my eyes, pulling on that connection I feel with the land and on the magic that's been brewing inside of me. When the two are called up, I push my intention into the mixture. This is not the way I was taught to do magic, but it feels right somehow. So, I let my instincts guide me.

And then, after I think it won't work, I see it.

I open my eyes slowly, "I know where we need to go."

CHAPTER 6

The fae don't question me. Derek pulls Julian up to a standing position once more and then I'm the one leading the way. The air around us grows heavier. The smoke and ash from the fires is dense enough that it's difficult to see past a few feet in front of us. It's hard not to cough, but we try to do our best. It wouldn't do us any good to give up our position. I'm hoping if we can't see the creatures, they can't see us.

After what seems like forever, I feel it. Pivoting to the left, I pick up speed. The smoke clears, and there it is.

"Avery?" Derek says, looking at the large house in front of us.

"We're going in."

"Are you sure that's a good idea?"

I glance over my shoulder. There's no hesitation in my voice when I reply, "Yes."

I think they'll argue further, but they don't.

The building is a two-story structure with an almost Grecian architecture to it. There are long columns of what was once white marble on each side of the door, as well as imbedded into the front beside the windows. Most of the windows are intact from what I can see, and they are long and narrow.

The door opens without a creak. I step in cautiously. The foyer opens up before me with a large staircase in the middle leading up to the second floor. Doorways are on each side of the foyer, leading to opposite side of the house.

I let my magic out, hoping it will tell me of any danger, but I don't feel anything specific. Granted, this is not something I've tried before, so I could be wrong. But I have to trust that the land lead me here for a reason. Looking over my shoulder, I motion the guys in.

Once inside the building, the air isn't much better. We deposit Julian against the wall in the foyer. I drop down to my knees next to him to assess the damage. He's bleeding pretty profusely, and it's not like I have a first aid kit with me. Wait, maybe I do.

I pull my bag forward. When I rummage through it, there are no antibiotics or bandages inside. I guess that's not something fae pack when they go on a long trip. And of course I didn't think about it either.

"I don't know how to help you," I tell him. He shakes his head looking up at Derek. I glance between the fae, furrowing my brow in confusion. "If you have something to say, gentlemen, then out with it." The number of secrets they keep from me is really astounding.

"It's not something I've done in ages," Derek comments, his full attention on Julian. It's like I'm not even there.

"I'm willing to take that risk."

The fae points to his jacket. The left arm is completely soaked through with his blood. I don't even know what we'll see when we take it off. I realize I need to find a way to at least clean it. Since no one is sharing information with me, I'll do what I can. We do have some water left over.

"Lean forward, Julian," I say, reaching for his jacket. He doesn't hesitate to obey. With his lips right over my shoulder, I hear his sharp intake of breath the moment he starts pulling his jacket off.

"The other side first," I say. Julian shrugs his arm out of the right sleeve, and then I gently move to help tug his left one off. The blood is heavy, making the material stick to his skin.

I have very basic first aid knowledge, just enough that I know it needs to be cleaned and pressure needs to be put on it, or it'll keep bleeding. It would be helpful to have one of the healer witches here now.

Julian jerks from the pain, and I stop pulling. "I'm sorry."

"Not your fault," he replies, his teeth clenched together. He's paler than even ten minutes ago, sweat dripping down the sides of his face. I manage to get the jacket completely off, and thankfully, he has a t-shirt underneath. His upper arm is a complete mess. I have to roll up the sleeve a little, but it looks exactly like what it is. That creature took a chunk out of his skin. The teeth marks are clearly displayed. I can see almost all the way down to his bone. It looks even worse than I imagined.

"Avery—"

"Is your blood...bubbling?" I reach over to touch it, but he catches my hand in his other one.

"Troll bites can be poisonous."

That nearly stops my breath right there.

"I don't think simple pressure is going to fix this," I say, my heart heavy with the idea of losing Julian. Knowing he could bleed out in my arms is almost too much to take.

"Isn't there some magic you fae have that will help fix this? No healing abilities?"

"Not unless you have shifter blood in you too, but even that is rare," Derek replies. That gives me another idea.

"Is there something I can do? I have shifter blood, right?"

"It doesn't work like that, Avery." Julian places a hand over my own, giving it a gentle squeeze.

"Don't do that," I snap, yanking my hand back. "Don't look like you're over here, saying your last goodbye. There has to be something." I don't miss the way his eyes slide over to Derek's for a second, so I jump to my feet. Something passed between them earlier, and they didn't want to go into it. Well, tough luck. We're getting into it now.

"You. There's something you can do. What is it?"

Derek doesn't move away as I march up to him. There are only a few feet between us. He gives me a cold look, which makes him more fae somehow, but I'm not intimidated. Maybe I should be. But I'm already dealing with a lot. I'm not about to deal with this crap either.

"What. Is. It?" I repeat, this time a little slower. "Should I act it out too, or can you understand the three simple words?"

His eyes flash in annoyance or anger, I'm not sure which. And I don't care.

"Your habit of keeping me out of the loop needs to end. Right here and now. Julian is dying. So, whatever it is that you *both*," I turn and glare at Julian, before looking back at Derek, "are keeping to yourself, isn't worth it. Not if it makes him lose his life."

"It's ancient magic, Avery. It's something the royal blood possesses, but it isn't exactly practiced," Derek says, his voice as cold as his eyes. There's more to it, of course. It's like pulling teeth with these two.

"Do you want Julian to die?"

There's a moment of silence where the only sound is our breathing and the drip of Julian's blood on the dark floor.

"I do not."

Three words, but they're the ultimate truth.

"Then, *do* something."

Derek gives me another long look before moving to kneel near Julian.

"Are you sure about this?" he asks, looking the other fae in the eye.

"Yes."

I'm not exactly sure what I'm witnessing, but then, Derek takes Julian's mangled arm into his hands and closes his eyes.

For a long time, nothing happens. It's the dormant part of the magic that's reawakening. I've heard of hidden or buried powers. Well, I also have one. So, I wait, even as Julian begins to breathe heavier.

Then a soft glow illuminates Derek. He seems to be glowing from the inside out. I hold my breath as I wait for whatever it is that's going to happen. The glow stays around Derek, and then, it seems to move into Julian. The moment it shifts, Julian screams.

I drop down beside him immediately, but I can't touch him. I don't want to make it worse, whatever is happening.

"Derek, you're hurting him."

"I have to."

Horrified, I watch as Derek pins Julian down. The screams of the fae echo all around us. Then the glow bursts out from inside of Julian's wound, and I fall back away from it. It seems to take forever, but Julian stops screaming, and the light goes out like a candle. He slumps down, completely knocked out as Derek sits back on his heels.

"Derek, is he..."

"He'll be fine. He just needs to rest."

Derek sounds like he's just run a marathon. When he stands, he doesn't meet my eye. He simply walks out of the room. Glancing over at Julian, I watch as his chest rises and falls. The sight of it makes me sigh in relief.

I stand and make sure Julian is laying down comfortably before I go and find Derek.

* * *

I find him in one of the rooms down the hall. There's still furniture there, although I don't think I'd want to sit on any of it. It's covered in enough dust and decay that it would crumple under a feather of a touch.

Derek is standing near one of the long, narrow windows, his

gaze on something outside. Not that he can see much. The ash and smoke have somehow gotten heavier.

"Are you okay?"

It's not the question I was going to ask, but it's out before I can stop it. I think I surprise him too. He turns to glance at me as I come up to stand beside him. I notice he's a bit sweaty too.

"I'm fine."

"Is that a real fine or a fine that will stop me from asking more questions?"

"Well, clearly the latter isn't working."

I smile a little, despite myself. There's a softness about him right now that I'm not sure what to do about.

The way he is surprises me on a daily basis. He's unlike everything I've ever learned about fae, and I'm not sure what to do with that information.

"It's been a long time since I've done that," Derek finally says, looking back out into the ashy forest.

"Can you tell me what you did?"

At first, I don't think he will.

"I transferred some of my essence into him. Shared a part of me."

"Wait, I don't understand. I've never heard of that before."

"It's from old magic. It's how the rulers gained their power. They had an ability to heal their people. Wouldn't you want a king on the throne who could do that?"

"You sound bitter."

"Maybe I am."

"Your mother." I don't even have to ask because I know that's what this is about. She's been the queen for a very long time, longer than my human brain can comprehend. She doesn't seem like someone who has ever healed anyone.

"She would never and has forbidden me to do so. When a part of the essence is transferred, a part of your time is given away. I feel tired right now, but that will go away with time."

"Wait, you mean, you'll die faster now?" My heart squeezes at the thought, but I try not to show it. I don't need him seeing just how much that distresses me. And I definitely will need to deal with those feelings as well. Anyway.

"No one knows how much time is given away. Fae live for a long time. A little shorter isn't so bad."

There's almost a touch of sadness in his voice, but I don't think he'll appreciate me catching that.

"Is that why you were reluctant to do it?"

There's another long pause before he turns to me and replies.

"No. Anytime I use my magic, the queen can tell. It's a spell—more like a curse—she put on me a long time ago. While I can prevent it when I'm in the human world, here? We're still in Faery. If she senses we're in the forbidden forest...it won't end well for us."

"She's tracking you?" When I think the fae have reached their limit on mind boggling, there's another tier. Derek nods, and I honestly don't even know what to feel about that. I have a hundred questions, but maybe now isn't the best time. I decide to change gears.

"You say we're in Faery, just in a different time."

"Yes."

"Could you explain that a bit better? If we're stuck in a time and place that's a future possibility, does anything we do affect...anything?" I ask, trying to wrap my mind around it all.

"No. It's the future. As long as we don't magically alter anything that can track back to the past, we'll be fine."

"That almost makes sense," I say, sighing. This place is giving me a headache. I'm not sure if it's the weird magic, or if it's just the heaviness of the place, but I'm ready to get out of here.

"So how do we return?"

"We need to find a portal ripple."

"Like the anomaly that swallowed us and brought us here in

the first place?" I throw my hands up in the air. "Of course, why wouldn't that be the way to go?"

"It won't be the same one. And…"

"What? Don't stop now."

"The ripples are many, which means, so are the timelines. We might not end up where we need to be right away."

"Cool. This is getting better by the minute."

"We'll get out of here, Avery." Derek's voice is full of conviction, and yes, I do believe him. Especially considering fae can't lie. But I'm still frustrated by the whole thing.

"I need a minute."

He opens his mouth to protest but then doesn't. Smart fae. He's learning.

The emotional weight of this place is really getting to me all of a sudden, so I leave Derek standing near the window and walk back out into the hallway.

I'm restless.

I'm confused.

I'm sad.

That last one is purely because of what I just learned about Derek. I don't want to keep feeling sympathy for the prince. Ever since I've known him, he's done things that are questionable. I'm sure he's done plenty of other things I don't want to know about as well. But somehow, I'm still drawn to him. To this side of him.

The protector.

And that's dangerous. I had to walk away from him, or I would've done something I regretted. I might have reached over to hold him close, somehow thinking my touch could protect him from his monster of a mother. Or maybe I want him to protect me from the reality of this place. I'm all over, up and down, side to side, trying to control all these emotions and thoughts.

It doesn't seem to be working.

CHAPTER 7

I end up upstairs. After checking to make sure Julian is still resting, I take the grand staircase to the second floor. I'm not really looking for anything specific. I just need a moment to clear my head.

Everything has been happening so fast, and the toll it's taking on me, it's not something I can even describe to myself.

One minute, I'm strong and ready to take on the world.

The next, I want to weep my heart out.

My mother would probably call it hormones. The shifter in me gets those mood swings really bad, especially in the early years. But this seems like more somehow.

I must find a way to keep a lid on the madness going on inside of me. There are creatures all around us that are waiting to pounce. Julian will hopefully wake up soon. Derek is—well, Derek. I need to get a grip on reality, or I'll be even more useless than I was in the forest with the boggarts.

I really do need to learn more fighting skills. Even with what Derek taught me at the cabin, I'm still too rusty to be of much use.

There are a few doorways in front of me, but none of them

seem to have doors. I chose one at random, curious about this place, but mostly just needing the space to wander.

The room is in shadows, only one window present on the opposite wall. There's also what seems to be a fog all around me. It reaches for me before I realize what's happening. There's a ripple and then I am through.

When I step out of the fog, my surroundings are completely different. Twisting around, I try to look back, but there's just a sheet of white behind me. The doorway is gone and so is the house.

"Derek! Julian!" I call out, but the only answer I receive is my own echo. I try to reach back through the white, but then even that disappears and now there's a forest there. Seeing no other option, I move forward.

The trees are no longer dying. The ground beneath my feet seems fresher somehow. This place feels just as dangerous as the wasteland I left behind, even though I don't smell the ground burning. It looks serene, but I know better than to trust that. Looks can be, and often are, deceiving.

These time jumps have to have a way out. I can't be stuck in this constant loop. A movement catches my attention, and I swerve in that direction immediately. I'm not about to call out a hello, but I will see if someone other than me is actually here.

The fog dissipates suddenly, and I find myself in a courtyard. It's similar to the one at Queen Svetlana's castle, but also different. The trees here are larger, reaching so high into the sky that I can't see them. Flowers bloom in the darkness, but they grow right out of the tree bark instead of the ground. The space around the trees is lost to the darkness, so I can't see the shape of it.

I move forward, but then stop. My feet are cocooned in some-thing. When I glance down, I find myself in a pink ball gown. My hands roam over my body to see if it's real, and it is. The skirt is full and cinched at the waist. The front is low cut, and my shoul-ders are bare. My hair is down, falling in soft waves over my back. I'm spotless, as if I didn't just come from a raging fire forest.

"You're here."

The voice snaps my head up, and I squint through the darkness to find the source of it. I know it, even without having to see him.

"Derek!" I pull up my skirt, rushing toward him as he seemingly materializes from the shadows. He's standing near a tree. When I reach him, the glow from the flowers illuminates his face. He's dressed in a dark blue suit, his hair tousled in that sexy way of his. He's just as clean as I am.

"I didn't think you'd show," he says when I stop in front of him. My brows furrow in confusion as I look at him. There's genuine emotion on his face, something that nearly takes my breath away. He is never so upfront about them. That's when I realize this is not the Derek of now. It's the Derek of whatever time this is.

And I'm not me either. I'm whoever he expects me to be, and I can't resist but to play along.

"Why did you think I wouldn't?"

He doesn't answer right away. His eyes do a slow sweep over my face before he glances down at the dress. When his eyes meet mine again, there's real appreciation in them, and it makes my chest hurt. Derek has never looked at me like this in real life. Or *my* real life I suppose. He takes a step forward, reaching for my hands. Taking both of them in his, he peers into my face, his eyes intense on mine.

"I know things haven't worked out how we planned them. But you have to know that everything I've done was to protect you. I would never—" The sadness in his eyes is almost tangible, and his grip on my hands is tight. "Killing them was the only way. You have to know that. They were holding you back. But no more. We can rule now. Their blood is on my hands, but her blood is on yours. We're the perfect match, don't you see? We're—"

"Stop!" I say, yanking my hands back and stepping away. I can't be hearing this. I can't be having this conversation with a future him because I don't know if this is my future or not. What he's saying, it doesn't make sense. And I don't want it to. I don't want to know we've become these evil beings. I can't hear this, because if I hear it and believe it, I will never trust him. And I can't afford to do this without trusting him.

"What is it? I'm sorry, Avery. I'm sorry that I—"

"It's not you." I stop him once more, almost laughing at the absurdity of me using that line. "This, this is all too much, and I have to get out of here."

I turn to flee because that is my only option. This is not my world. This is not my Derek, and I have to get back to both of them. Now.

He calls my name again, but I don't stop. The dress is heavy around my legs, but I keep moving. There's no direction in my mind to go, just away. I hear more movement behind me and turn to see a group of guards rushing after me. I trip over the skirt, falling forward, my hair in my face. Any second now the guards will descend.

But when I glance up, I'm back in the room I was just in. Glancing around quickly, I make sure nothing has come through the ripple with me. Although, I don't even know if that was a ripple. It was so fast and unexpected.

And Derek. He looked so—no, I'm not thinking about that right now.

Push it all down, Avery. You have to find a way to get out of here.

* * *

WE DON'T GO FARTHER into the house than the foyer. When I make it back downstairs, Derek is sitting on the floor, opposite of Julian. His eyes are on me when I walk over to check on Julian, and they are still on me as I settle against the wall near the staircase.

I want to tell him about what happened upstairs, but I also don't. If he decides to go up there, I'll warn him. But for now, I'm going to keep the experience to myself. I'm not even sure it was real. It felt way too disorienting. It wasn't like the ripple we came through to get here. It was more like a waking vision, something the Ancients have done before to talk to me. It didn't feel like them, but I really don't know, do I?

"I'll take the first watch," I say. The way his eyes flash, I know I beat him to it. But he doesn't argue. Maybe it's because he knows his body needs the rest after the transfer. I watch him as he closes his eyes, and then, as his body relaxes.

Thankfully, the whole night goes by without incident. When Derek wakes me up, I feel slightly rested. He kneels over me, his hand gentle on my shoulder. When I look up at him, there's genuine care there.

The flashes of his sad eyes from my vision—or whatever it was —mixed with the reality in front of me, and the desire to hold him, nearly overwhelms me. Instead, I push to a sitting position as he moves back.

"She awakens."

My gaze jerks over to Julian who is sitting up now and looking very peppy. I jump to my feet, rushing over to him.

"You're okay?"

"I'm okay."

I still do a thorough once over and notice that his wound is almost completely scabbed over. Glancing at Derek, I make sure he's fine as well because it must've taken a lot of his magic to make that happen.

We don't linger around after that. Grabbing my bag, we leave through the same door we entered, but we don't go back in the same direction. I let Derek take the lead, with Julian between us, and me bringing up the rear.

I still feel her, the land around me. She's so sad. She's been through so much. Maybe, in some strange way, I relate to her on that level. We've both been put into a situation we didn't chose for ourselves.

Julian calls for a rest mid-morning. We stop, taking a drink and eating some of the fruit from my bag.

"Will I jinx it if I say it's been awfully quiet?" I ask. The fae look at me a little confused. So maybe that's more of a human thing than not.

"It has, but we just might be in an area of the forest that's less populated for some reason," Derek replies. I have to keep myself from smiling. He sounds so serious when I was trying to lighten things up.

"Do you think I can try that magic trick I did to find the house?" I ask, but both of the fae are already shaking their heads.

"It's dangerous to keep doing it. We don't know how it'll affect you or the land around us. This isn't our Faery."

I think part of the side effects was that strange trip I went on, but I'm not about to mention it. It's not like I could replicate what I did anyway. It was all instinct. I'm too much in my head right now to allow my magic to take over.

"Derek, do you actually have any idea where we're going?" I ask, instead of voicing all of my own concerns. He stays quiet for a moment before turning to look over his shoulder at me.

"The only sure thing I know is that no matter where we are in Faery, north is the true direction. So, if we go north here, maybe we'll get somewhere." The *I'm-not-sure* part is silent. We're all just guessing at this point.

"I didn't think the true north nursery rhyme was true," I comment as we begin walking again. Both Derek and Julian glance over at me, but it's Julian who asks.

"Nursery rhyme?"

"Sure. All the kids know the story of the little spider." They continue looking at me like I've lost my mind. I guess fae don't tell the same stories to their children as witches do. I'm not surprised.

I can't see someone like Queen Svetlana teaching little Derek about the dangers of walking alone at night.

"There were a few I remember from childhood. Each little rhyme is a story, and it teaches you an important lesson. I always thought the spider one was about resilience and how you can overcome whatever is thrown at you if you only try, but maybe not."

"Can we hear it?" Derek's question is barely above a whisper, as if he wanted to ask but didn't actually want me to hear it. I smile, the fae curiosity is such an interesting thing.

"There once was a spider, who traveled alone.
He lived in the rafters and called darkness his home.
But one day, a storm came, and blew the spider away,
He spun and he spun, then, in a forest he lay.

The spider was scared and lost as can be,
But he knew that true north would guide him, you see.
He followed the signs, and he followed the sun,
And one day he came to his new-found home.

It wasn't the rafters, and he wasn't alone,
For he found his lost family and he no longer had to roam."

The simple words bring another smile to my face because these were the simple days. It reminds me of when I would spend time with my parents and didn't have to worry about some great destiny or powers beyond my imagination. I was still an outcast, half shifter and half witch, but I was loved and protected. I was happy.

"It's an odd rhyme," Julian comments, breaking my trip down memory lane.

"Maybe, but rhymes such as these stick in your mind and are fun as a kid." I shrug because I think this is where I learned to love knowledge. It's why I wanted to become a Watcher, because I wanted to know things.

"It is true though," Derek says from his place in front of us. "True north is a guiding point in Faery. It's interesting that your parents taught you that rhyme."

His words and the way he says them makes me pause. I try to remember if anyone else spoke that rhyme then or in the years since, and I can't think of anyone. There were a bunch of rhymes that my parents made up just for me, and now, it makes sense.

"You think my dad was preparing me." It's not a question, but Derek stops anyway and turns to face me.

"I think he was."

I don't know how to take that, and I don't want their sympathy right now. Pushing past Derek, I continue walking, picking up speed. Suddenly, the trees in front of me open up. We're in a clearing. The guys come up to stand on each side of me as we take in the scene in front of us.

"It can't be."

$\mathcal{W}$e move forward, making sure to hurry across the open space.

"I don't understand," I say as I study our surroundings. My brow is furrowed. "What is this? It looks—it looks like Thunderbird Academy. But—"

"Destroyed"

I glance at Derek at that one word as we stop in front of where the side door used to be. It leads to the now-non-existent gardens.

The school is in ruins. Half of the walls are missing, brick laying in piles, as if an actual bomb went off in there. We step over the rubble, keeping our eyes peeled.

The ever-changing dynamic of this world is dangerous. The air here is clearer, as if the ash and smoke hasn't reached this far. Except, this place looks like it's been right in the middle of a war.

"What do you think happened here?" I can't help but ask.

The guys don't answer right away. I look over to find Derek staring at something on the ground. He seems a million miles away from here and then he snaps back.

"The Ancients got through the wards and destroyed everything in sight. Look at the scorch marks." Derek points to what's left of the wall in from of him, and I can see them now. Black stains of magic curl around the hole that's been created. The grass around the walls is dead as well. It's the aftermath of a powerful magic battle. Nothing will ever grow here again.

"They fought back," I mumble because I know they did. Thunderbird Academy is one of the greatest magical schools in our world. People that I've looked up to my whole life have graced these halls with their presence. They learned here, and they taught here. It was the school that I worked hard to get into to.

Before finding that stupid book changed everything for me.

"This can happen? It's a possible future?" I ask the questions, but in reality, of course it can happen. I know this already. It's why I came to Faery in the first place. I need to learn to use the magic that's been bestowed upon me. The fear that I'll fail is more over-powering here as I stand amidst the ruins of the school I love so much.

"There are many possibilities, Avery," Derek replies, clearly seeing my distress. He comes to stand in front of me, as if he's blocking the ruins from view. I'm forced to look up into his handsome face.

"Nothing you see here is set in stone. This is just one outcome, one out of thousands. Every decision we make in our own time affects what happens here. So, we make a decision not to let this happen."

"It's not that easy, Derek, and you know it," I whisper, all of the emotions creeping up on me at once. "I'm responsible for the outcomes because I'm the one who can read an ancient book no one else can. This will be on me."

"It will be on all of us. If this happens, we failed all of Faery."

I want to believe him, I want to share that responsibility, but the whole land and its people are dependent on me. Just then, something dawns on me.

"Wait, if we're in Faery, how is the school here?" Thunderbird

Academy is in the human realm. It's been to Faery before, but Maddie fixed that problem.

"The Ancients must've opened up a rift between the realms with their magic. Everything would be confused if that happened. Or maybe this is a future where the school never made it back to the human realm."

I remember them mentioning before how the Ancients can mess with dimensions and realities, but here's a visual representation of it. I don't like it. I don't like any of this one bit.

The sadness I felt for the land itself is intensified here by my own emotions. I want to take the pieces of this broken school, and put them together, brick by brick. If only fixing everything was as easy as that sounds.

I open my mouth to ask more questions when a noise catches my attention. The fae turn as one, their own focus on whatever it is we're hearing.

"Get down." Derek grabs my arm and pulls me down beside him. We're right on the other side of the wall with the hole blown through it. Julian drops down a few yards away from us. Derek pokes his head up, still staring at the forest right at the edge of the clearing. I'm about to say I don't see anything when a group of the deformed trolls burst out of the trees.

* * *

WE STAY AS STILL as possible as the trolls move across the clearing. They're speaking a language I don't understand. I'm almost afraid to breathe lest I get their attention. There's a lot of land around the school, and they seem to be on a mission to get somewhere.

It seems like forever, but it's is only probably a minute before they disappear into the trees on the other side of the school. Yet, we still don't move. I'm back to feeling overwhelmed. And sad. This land is really playing up on the sadness, and I don't blame her. She's been through so much.

"Avery?" Derek's voice reaches out to me, as if through a tunnel. I look up to meet his concerned gaze. He looks blurry.

That's when I realize I'm crying again. I really have no control over the emotions the land evokes in me, or my response to it.

The sobs seem to burst out of me as I try my best to keep the sound down. Sadness overpowers every thought in my mind. I have no control over my reaction to it. I feel it; I feel it all. The torture the land has endured, the terror of the burning fields and the rotting trees, I feel everything. No one is here to sympathize with her, no one is here to comfort her.

The land bleeds, and she feels so alone.

Suddenly, strong arms pull me forward. I fall against Derek's chest as he cocoons me in his embrace. I grab onto his shirt, clinging to him like he's my lifeline, while the waves of sadness try to overwhelm me. One of Derek's hands threads through the hair at the back of my head, pulling me even closer. I breathe him in, surrounded by him on every side.

My body shakes with tears, but he doesn't let go. His other hand makes slow trails up and down my back, soothing my worries away. I give myself over to the feelings. I let the land know that she's not alone. That I'm—we—are doing everything we can to help her. It takes a few moments, but I finally feel the land's power drain out of me, giving me my emotions back. After another minute, I'm in control.

Pulling away, I look up to find Derek staring down at me.

"Avery?" There's so much in just that word and the look on his face.

"I'm really ready to get out of here," I reply, wiping at my tearstained cheeks. Derek nods, but he doesn't take his eyes off me. There's so much emotion there, it's the most earnest I've seen him since we've met. If we weren't us, and if we were in another place and time, I think I could stay in the circle of his arms for forever.

"Guys, we have to move." Julian's voice reaches us, and we both turn to see what causes the alarm in his voice. He's looking out through the torn-up wall. When we follow his gaze, we see them. The trolls have come back.

"They probably heard me—"

"Let's just get out of here."

Derek takes my hands, pulling me up beside him, and then we're running. Julian keeps pace beside us. We have no direction in mind, just away. The trees are in front of us, the ruined Thunderbird Academy behind us, and the trolls coming at us from all directions.

"We can't outrun them!" Julian shouts. I twist my head to glance over my shoulder. They're so much closer and faster than I thought. He's right. They don't leap like other creatures, but they move fast, and we're not moving fast enough.

"Try and lose them in the trees!" Derek commands right as we hit the tree line. Since the air here is cleaner, it's easier to see where we're going. But that means the trolls can see us just as well.

There's nothing I can do. I brought this on us, and now, we're probably going to die in this wasteland before we have a chance to do anything good. The sound of trolls yapping is closing in. I'm out of breath. My only thought is to stop them. Somehow. Someway.

Determination fuels me as I stop running and turn to face them head on. I hear Derek and Julian yell my name the moment they realize I'm not with them, but I have to try this.

Giving myself completely over to my instincts, I don't think. I thrust my hands out in front of me, calling on my magic and the land which I'm so connected to, trusting both of them to guide me.

A burst of fire rushes out of my palms, igniting everything in sight. It sweeps the trolls off their feet. But then, something unusual happens. My left palm becomes a stream of water, enveloping the trolls and drowning them on dry land.

It all happens so fast, I don't have any time to think about it. The wings burst out of my back for a split second, sending the space around me into brightness before they're gone. But I don't give up. I let the magic pour out of me until I have nothing left.

Then, it's done. The fire and water disappear, and the trolls vanish with them. Derek and Julian are beside me, but it's Derek who catches me when I fall. There is no strength left in my body, not an ounce of it enough to hold me up. Derek cradles me against his chest, picking me up off the ground.

No one says a word, as I lean against Derek's strong chest, completely spent. The boys turn, and when they do, a shimmer appears in front of us. I know it's what we've been looking for.

"Thank you," I whisper. The shimmer becomes bigger and then it pulls us in.

CHAPTER 9

*T*he light disappears and then I'm looking at the most beautiful sight I've ever seen. The trees that surround us are fully green. They are big and strong and healthy.

"We're back," Julian says, breathing out a sigh of relief. It's not a question because we all know it's true. The heaviness of being in the forbidden forest is back, but also, this feels like home.

Home.

I never thought of Faery as a place I would ever call home, but in that wasteland, I took ownership of the land and called it mine. I don't think that will ever change now.

"But how?" This time it is a question. Derek lifts me a little higher, to get a better grip on me as I fight to stay awake.

"I think it was me," I mumble, closing my eyes and basking in his body's warmth. I feel safer than I have in a long time now, and it has everything to do with who is holding me.

"I think you're right," Derek says. I know he's looking down at me because his voice sounds closer. A moment later, I feel his breath on my face, and I smile. Or maybe it's only internally, because I don't think I'm strong enough to even manage that right now.

"Rest, Avery. You're safe."

There's nothing else that I can say to that, and a moment later, I'm no longer awake.

The forest is dark around me when I open my eyes. My back is leaning against a tree, and I'm using my arm as a pillow. Sitting up slowly, I look for Derek and Julian, but they're nowhere in sight. Something stops me from calling out to them. I'm not sure what exactly it is that I'm feeling. There's a heaviness around me that has nothing to do with the forest itself.

"You are here and so are we." The voice is sudden, and I jump, as it sounds like it comes from all around me. I get to my feet, spinning in circle as I try to find the source of it, but I don't see anything.

"You are here and so are we, and you will not escape."

The words get louder and louder as they are spoken and then,

"You will not escape. You will not escape. You will not escape."

I jerk into wakefulness, and it's only Derek's arms that keep me from falling. He's still holding me as close as he can. He's visibly concerned when I look up into his handsome face.

"Bad dream," I mumble, unable to look away from him. He's been letting me see these glimpses of vulnerability, and I'd be lying to myself if I said I don't find myself wanting to know more. No matter how much my brain tells me to keep him at arms-length, I can't seem to want to do anything but pull him closer.

"Can I get down?" I ask, even though it's the last thing I want to do. But I seem to have regained my strength, and I don't want to be a burden.

"Are you sure?"

No.

"Yes."

He stops walking, setting me down carefully, keeping his arm around my waist in case I need it. I seem to be steady on my feet. I wonder how long I've been asleep. So, I ask.

"About half a day," Julian replies, coming up to stand beside me.

"What?" I glance between the two fae, completely confused. "It couldn't have been that long."

"It was."

Derek carried me for half a day? And he carried me while in a forest that makes everything heavier and darker? I study his face, but he's back to wearing his princely mask. The frustration at seeing it makes me forget my impulse to thank him. So instead, I only nod.

"We're heading north, I assume?"

"We are," Derek replies, turning on his heels and taking the lead. It's like nothing has even happened between us. He's back to his cold fae self. He's moodier than I can deal with right now, so I ignore the snide remark I want to deliver.

"I'm glad you're better," Julian says, falling into step beside me as we follow Derek. I smile at him, bumping his shoulder with mine. After a few moments, he falls back to bring up the rear, and I veer off to the right a little. I've been with these two for days now, I think maybe my mind is just confused. We've been in life and death situations, it's only natural I feel connected to them.

Nothing else.

"Avery, watch out." Julian doesn't shout, but there's enough alarm in his voice to stop me in my tracks.

"What?" I look around but don't see anything out of the ordinary. The forest is just as heavy around us as it was, the eerie silence a bit more pronounced.

"We're almost there, so we have to tread carefully. There's illusion magic in place."

His explanation does nothing to clarify the confusion, but my magic has other ideas. The moment Julian say illusion, it's like the faery magic inside of me decides to wake up. Immediately, I start to feel things. I can feel the ground beneath my feet, the moisture clinging to the leaves, the sturdiness of the trunks. And then, a dozen yards to the left, I feel something else.

"This way," I announce and shift to the left. The boys exchange a confused look, but I push past them and toward whatever it is in front of me.

"Maybe we should—"

But I'm not listening. Now that I've found the anomaly, my magic is pulling me toward it. When I stop, there's nothing but trees in front of me, but I can feel it. There's a disturbance in the air.

Tentatively, I reach out with my hand, placing my palm against nothing. For a moment, nothing happens. Then the air ripples, and it's like a curtain is opened. I blink, pulling my hand back quickly before I focus on what lies beyond. It's a large house, more like a mansion, with a tree growing out of the south end of it.

The front door is adorned by large columns, and in the next moment, it swings open. My jaw drops as I watch the person step out into the light.

"Well, it's about time," Hannah says, her signature smirk on her lips.

* * *

"HANNAH?"

The guys move toward the mansion, but I stay frozen, completely confused. Derek realizes this right away and drops back.

"Avery?"

"I don't understand. This was your big secret? Your way to teach me about my magic? You decided to send me to the person who could've helped me in the beginning and didn't."

"I understand you're angry—"

"I'm furious. I thought I'd finally have some answers, but no. You fae just have to play with me."

Derek's face completely drops at my accusation before he catches himself. His momentary lapse pauses my rant. I hurt him. Somehow, with something that I said, I actually hurt him.

And then it hits me. I called him fae. I threw him in the same category as his mother and everyone else who would like to manipulate me, which, let's be honest, is a huge list at this point.

"Derek—"

"Hannah will help. She will. We wouldn't be here otherwise."

His voice is sure, and when he meets my eye, there's determination there. If nothing else, I can trust that he believes this. So, I will give it a shot.

"You shouldn't be mad at the poor boy, Avery. I wasn't going to help you until I was ready," Hannah says as we reach the front doors. She's wearing another one of her maxi dresses, this one a different shade of red. It covers about as much as a bathing suit, her back, shoulders, and most of her legs bare as she motions us in.

Once inside, I see Julian hugging another guy about a few years older than me. When they pull back, I notice that he looks like a blonder version of Julian.

"Avery, this is Jerome. My brother."

"Nice to meet you," I say, looking from Julian to Jerome. He never mentioned he had a brother. I wonder if that's what drove him to find a better life, or not. Sometimes family is the best motivator.

"You must be tired, and you all could use a shower, that's for sure. You boys know where to go. I'll take Avery with me."

When Derek doesn't move, Hannah levels him with a look.

"I'll take good care of her. Now go."

He gives me a fiery look and then turns and follows Julian and Jerome out of the main hall.

"He's protective of you."

"He knows he's in trouble," I throw back, turning to face the woman in front of me. She's wearing her signature smirk as she looks at me. I try not to squirm under her gaze.

"You really did it, Avery. You made it all that time away from this place, and now, here you are."

"Didn't have much of a choice. It's not like I had anyone to help me."

Hannah's laugh rings out as she pivots and heads in the opposite direction of the boys.

"I've forgotten how clever you can be."

"Wasn't trying to be. Just stating the truth."

"Ah, yes. The truth. Curious that someone with fae blood in her has the ability to...bend it." She stops in front of double doors, giving me another once over before pushing them open.

"I don't know what you want me to say," I begin before I fully see the room we walked into. It's gorgeous. Sure, the room at the palace is too, but this one feels more personable.

The walls are pearl white with a gold trim at the top and the bottom. The bed is on my right, in the middle of the wall, with space on each side. A tulle white canopy hangs over it. When I look closely, it's full of tiny sparkling stars. There's a dresser, a table, a door to what I assume is the bathroom. But what I love most about the room are all the plants.

There are geometrical shelves covering the wall opposite the bed that are filled with various plants. Vining and flowering, they spread out like a work of art. There are vases on every surface and more shelves on the various walls. The room is full of light and oxygen, and it makes me smile.

"I knew you'd like it."

"It's very—modern." I think that's why I love it on sight. True, the room at the palace was straight out of every royalty movie or period drama. But this? It has a different type of a beauty. It reminds me of home.

Hannah doesn't comment on that, but it seems like she's pleased. She motions toward the open door before turning back to me.

"Get cleaned up. There are clothes in the closet or the dresser. Choose anything that strikes your fancy." I glance up at that, and she smiles. "We'll have dinner in a few, shall we?"

She moves toward the door, leaving me still gaping at my surroundings.

"Hannah?" I call out as she pulls the door open. The thank you is on the tip of my tongue, but I swallow it. Instead, I focus on more present issues. "Do you have it?"

"Of course I do."

CHAPTER 10

*O*nce we've all cleaned up, we end up in a large library. Being surrounded by all the books makes me feel better instantly. I took a shower, and my hair is wet and falling down my back. I brushed it out few times, taking my time with it. I didn't think such a small thing could make me feel so much better. The golden veins are still wrapped around my ear, but nothing feels different. The green streaks in my hair haven't gotten more pronounced. I think this is just part of my look now.

Derek is standing at the opposite wall while Julian and Jerome are seated in two of the chairs. I walk over to the love seat as Hannah gives me a quick once over.

"I knew the clothes would fit."

I glance down at the leggings and oversized sweatshirt I found in the dresser. They're so completely opposite of the gorgeous dress she's wearing, but I needed a sense of normalcy in my life right now. This feels cozy enough to let me pretend.

"Let's do this then."

Hannah walks over to the bookshelf, pulling out one of the leather-bound books. I know what she's about to show me, even though the guys don't. She opens the book and pulls out two unattached pieces of paper.

"Is that?" Julian asks, glancing from Hannah to me and back at Hannah.

"It is."

The woman walks over to where I'm sitting and takes the other side of the love seat as she settles beside me. She hands me the two pieces of paper. The moment my hands touch the parchment, a rush of magic goes through me.

Derek, Julian, and Jerome all move forward, fascinated by the papers I'm now holding in my hands. They stare at them like they've never seen anything like them. I smile as I thrust the papers toward them with a little "Boo". The guys jump, and I don't bother to suppress my chuckle.

"It doesn't bite, you know," I say, presenting them with the papers to take them. At first, I don't think they will, but then both Julian and Derek reach for a page. They hold them reverently, and that's expected. The pages are older than they are and the biggest part of their heritage.

"You can really read it?" Julian asks, staring at the page in his hand. The writing is there, but from what I understand, the fae just see gibberish. I'm the only person in generations who has looked at the pages and seen actual words. Sometimes there are also drawings and graphs of sorts.

Before I hid the book, I looked through as much of it as I could. It was difficult to study it, since I couldn't actually read it. Physically, I could. But I didn't want to accidentally start a world war or something if I mumbled a word out loud. Which I have been known to do when I study.

"It looks just like any book to me," I reply honestly. It seems to completely boggle their minds, and it's not like I can explain it any better.

"Boys, could you give me a moment alone with Avery?" Hannah asks, but we all know it's not a request. The guys don't hesitate to obey. Derek stops at the doorway, giving me a long look before glancing over at Hannah. Something seems to pass between them, and then he's gone.

"You're angry with me," Hannah begins, not beating around the bush. I turn to face her. She's seated just a foot away from me on the couch.

"Yes, I am." I don't hesitate to reply. "You left me floundering in the big bad world and for what? Clearly, you could've helped me from the beginning."

"Clearly, I could not."

"I don't believe that. Nothing has changed since I found that book. Well, maybe I have. But you? You're helping now, why?"

She stands, as if she needs distance to orient her thoughts. I don't push, waiting for her to speak up. She rearranges the hair over her shoulder before she finally does.

"This place is a sanctuary for me. Here in Faery, we do not have much say when it comes to what master we serve. If Queen Svetlana found out I was helping you...let's just say it wouldn't end well for me."

"Then why do it?"

"I was honest with you at Thunderbird Academy, Avery. I wanted you to have a choice. Faery is important to me. I want to see it not only survive, but to thrive. There are those in power who wouldn't care about the last one. It should not be so."

The words come out a little more intense than I think she intends for them to, and that's how I know she means it. There's real passion in her. She's not the nonchalant fae tutor that I met at the school. She believes in her homeland, and that, I can under-stand. That is why I decide to tell her when things changed for me.

"I connected with...her," I say, glancing down at the pages on my lap.

"Faery?"

"Yes. When we were in the other time." I look up to see her nod at me to continue. The guys must've filled her in. "I felt her sadness, her brokenness. I never thought a land could be so alive."

"But she is, and she must be protected," Hannah replies, walking back over to the seat. "Avery, I know you have no reason to trust any of us. Every single person, besides Jerome, has failed or lied to you. But you have to understand that our intentions were true."

"That doesn't make them right."

"No, it doesn't. But I hope you will give us the benefit of the doubt. We're fae...but we're trying."

I stay silent for a full minute, letting that sink in. It's the closest to an apology that I will ever get. I suppose I can continue being angry at her for leaving me alone when I needed someone the most, but that won't do me any good. I need her help. At the least.

"Okay, then keep trying," I say. She flashes a brilliant smile my way.

"Let's go to dinner and see if we can come up with a plan," she says. We both stand to leave. I place the papers on the table, but then I pick them back up again. I don't think I want them out of my sight. Hannah watches me but doesn't say anything, and then she leads the way out of the room.

* * *

THE NEXT FEW days go by in a blur. I learn that this house was setup as a sanctuary many centuries ago, before the forbidden forest was what it is now. Every realm has a version of one of these, something I didn't think about. Hannah was entrusted with the keep of it, but she wouldn't say by whom. It doesn't matter anyway.

What matters is that we are safe here from Queen Svetlana. Even Derek's magic can't be tracked when we're inside of the illusion bubble. That's what I've been calling it. They're not big fans of the name, but oh well. I kind of like it.

I'm not here to please anyone.

I'm here to learn.

That's why Jerome is here, apparently. He's older than Julian, probably around the same age as Nora, and he has a water affinity with magic. Hannah has created a training schedule for me. In other words, they're making a soldier out of me. It's not that I'm protesting, but no one consulted me first. I won't say thank you, even though I'm pretty sure I have to be just that to survive whatever is coming.

I still haven't told anyone about the dream I had. Maybe keeping all these things to myself isn't the best, but it's what I feel is best right now. At least, I keep reminding myself of that daily. I'm trying to learn how to trust the fae, but I cannot give it over completely. No matter what. I'm not sure if it's just my self-preserving instincts or what. But it is what it is right now.

This morning, I'm with Jerome at the back of the house. There's a fountain here, an angel with wings holding out his hands as water pours out of them. Fae are as close to nature as one can get, even more connected than witches. Still, most don't have active powers like elemental witches anymore. From everything I've heard, it's a power play from the royals. Fae can affect nature but don't use the elements in the same way.

Except Derek, of course. He has a lot of tricks up his sleeve.

And Jerome, who is half witch, so it helps him understand the dynamics.

"Can I ask you a personal question?" I begin when it's just the two of us. Hannah came out to give him some instructions, and Derek glared from the doorway. He hasn't been alone with me since we arrived. I'm not sure what caused the change in his behavior, but he does have a tendency to be hot and cold so maybe I should just get used to it by now.

"Ask away." Jerome doesn't hesitate.

"Do many fae have mixed culture parents?" I tried to make it sound as politically correct as possible, and that doesn't escape Jerome. He laughs, a full hearty laugh, before he replies.

"Yes, fae really can't keep it in their pants. And everyone has multiple children."

"Everyone?" I can't help my mind flying to Derek. And even Julian.

"Okay, not everyone," he laughs again, clearly catching my train of thought. "But in my case, my mother is a witch, but Julian's is fae."

"So, he doesn't have the elemental powers you do."

"I'm sure he would if he was taught to use them. Fae are more powerful than they let on. It's a special kind of a tactic."

"Don't I know it," I mumble, and Jerome chuckles. Everything is so calculated here. It's not that I don't appreciate precision, but this is definitely another level. I do like Julian's brother. He's very nonchalant about everything. He reminds me of the fae I met at Thunderbird Academy. I think having a human mother, or father, really makes a difference for these boys.

"Let's get started."

I sober up instantly. I've been able to access my water magic twice in the wasteland and neither time it was something I could control. I need to find a way to call on it, like I do my fire, but the usual ways aren't working for me. Even though Derek and I trained at the cabin, it's like I've forgotten how to do all of it. But it doesn't matter. Derek really has thought of everything.

I overheard him and Hannah talking yesterday, and it really was all him. He planned Hannah and Jerome both coming here and made it happen. He's been the one plotting behind everyone's back. I honestly have no idea how to feel about that. But at the moment, I'm grateful.

"When you access your fire magic," Jerome's voice brings me back to attention, "what do you feel?"

"Feel?"

"Yes. Is there a specific emotion that overwhelms you?"

I think about it, going over the times I have called upon it. Then, I do it in front of Jerome, letting the fire ignite in the palm of my hand before I shake my head.

"Nothing specific. I know this magic. I know the fire will come when call it." He's nodding before I even finish talking.

"I think that's what we focus on today. You getting to know the water magic. Get in."

"I'm sorry, what?"

Jerome points to the fountain again and says, "Get in."

"What do you—"

"Lay down on your back and see if you can float. I want you to be as submerged as you can. Then I need you to feel the water around you and in you because you are connected to it, even if you don't know it."

I stare at him for another moment, before I shrug my jacket, boots, and socks off. Left in my t-shirt and leggings, I step into the water, expecting it to be cool. But it's nice. It's a nice lukewarm, and when I lay down in it, it feels nice.

Following Jerome's instructions, I let myself float as I close my eyes.

"You know that magic responds to emotion, and you and this new magic have no emotional connection besides the few times you've been in danger. So, let yourself relax, let yourself feel, and meet the magic inside of you."

My body doesn't hesitate to follow the flow of his words. I don't think about it, don't think about my fire magic. I just give myself over to the water covering my skin, and I let it in.

I'm not sure how long I float like this until Jerome speaks up again.

"Avery, open your eyes."

When I do, there are droplets of water in the air above me, and I smile.

CHAPTER 11

That night, I leave the fae behind and walk out to the back of the house on my own. The illusion bubble reaches a dozen yards past the fountain, and I'm not really going anywhere farther than that. Slowly, I walk over to a dark spot in the grass, and lay down, giving myself time away from the prying eyes of the fae. I truly feel like they are watching me twenty-four-seven.

My fingers dig into the earth, connecting with it immediately. The connection I felt in the wasteland hasn't gone away. This Faery is just as connected to me as the future one was. But then again, they are one and the same. She welcomes me in. Closing my eyes, I trust this moment in time as I truly relax.

I never feel like I can do that in front of the fae. I always have to have my game face on.

Pretending.

Acting.

Masquerading.

It's becoming second nature to me. If that isn't the most fae thing, I don't know what is. I want to be better than what I know about them. I guess the books I've read only teach the ruthlessness. It's not that my companions haven't done questionable things. But so far, they've mostly been on my side. It's a strange combination of information.

I'm not sure how long I stay like that, just connected to the earth around me, but it refuels me somehow. Finally, I sit up, ready to go inside, when something changes.

The space around me dims, as if someone is turning down the lights, and shadows play against the backdrop. I get to my feet and spin in place, trying to find the source of the sudden change. That's when I notice the house is gone.

"Hello, child."

This time, I turn slowly. When I do, the same robed creature from the previous dream stands but ten feet in front of me. The space round him is even darker, as if he carries his own shadows within him.

"Where am I?"

"Still where you are. Yet, not at all. But we must talk."

Well, that made lots of sense. It's hard not to panic, but I push it down as much as I can. It would do me no good, losing my cool in front of this...creature.

"You have come to Faery. It was unexpected."

"Didn't you want me here?" Maybe I'm braver than I give myself credit for because the question escapes before I can think too much about it.

"We have many plans for you."

I wait for him to continue, but he doesn't.

"That's not cryptic at all," I comment, holding on to every ounce of courage I have in my blood.

"There are forces at play here, much bigger than you can imagine. Your power can open doors that have been shut for generations."

"Yes, I've heard," I mumble.

"There are books hidden within this land that even the queen has no knowledge about."

That perks up my attention. Queen Svetlana really makes it seem like she's all knowing. Granted, there are other queens in faery, but I have a feeling the creature speaks about all of them at once.

"Is that why you're here? You want me to find them?"

"We know where they are."

Then it clicks. They know, but they can't get to them.

"They're inside Faery, somewhere you can't get to."

My voice carries a tone of satisfaction, and it does not go unnoticed. The creature grows in size in front of me, a menacing growl escaping from inside those robes.

"We are unstoppable. Sometime soon, we will be in Faery."

"Then what do you need me for?" My voice shakes just a bit, but it's enough to placate the creature. He shrinks down a little, to appear more...approachable? It's the only reason I see for him to be playing these games. He goes from intimidating to approachable, looking for which one fits more for the situation.

"You can save us time by opening the Faery doors."

It sounds like an afterthought and a command at the same time. It turns my blood cold. The Ancients are more powerful than anything, and I have no doubt they'll break through. But if they're looking to use me, it means they're getting impatient. That never looks good on anyone, least of all a powerful magical entity.

"And if I don't?" I'm terrified of the answer and have every right to be.

"Then we will do whatever it takes to change your mind."

Just like that, he's gone. I'm shaking now, the possibilities endless in my mind. The air around me clears, and I'm once again standing at the back of the house, but this time, I find no calmness here.

Only horror.

* * *

71

"You're not paying attention," Derek says, his voice low. I glance at him, wiping the sweat from my eyes. We've been outside for about thirty minutes, and I'm already exhausted. Granted, I woke up exhausted because I barely slept. The visit from the Ancients has left me completely unbalanced. Clearly, they appear only to me and don't break any barriers or sound any alarms because no one even noticed.

"I'm doing the best I can."

"Then do better."

I narrow my eyes at him and his tone. He's been standoffish from the moment we got to Hannah's, and I'm sick of it.

"How about you do better? Better at explaining what you want me to do? Better at treating me like a normal human being?"

"You're not normal."

"No duh."

I'm angry, and I'm taking it out on him. Mentally, I know this. But emotionally, I would like to punch him. That's perfect since he's trying to teach me hand to hand combat. Even though we've done this before, I need way more practice than I'd like to admit.

Twice, we've been in a hand-to-hand battle, and I was pretty much useless. Yes, I have my magic...when it works. But that's not going to help if it decides to fritz on me. I absolutely cannot afford that, considering the Ancients are now making indirect threats toward my family. Because of course they are. Why wouldn't they? They will do whatever it takes to reach their goal. I should take some notes on their tenacity.

"Avery."

"What?"

"You're doing it again."

I drop my hands to my hips and face Derek head on. In turn, he folds his arms over his chest, his muscles bulging, but I won't be swayed. We stare at each other for a long moment, and I swear I can hear the air around us electrify. There I go again with my romantic notions. I need to stop thinking anything remotely close to romance when it comes to this fae, but there's just something about him.

Focus, Avery.

Focus.

Focus.

"Doing what exactly?" I finally ask, raising an eyebrow.

"You're a hundred miles away. You have to be present. If you're not, it's easy to sneak up on you."

Just then, Julian appears from seemingly nowhere, grabbing me around the middle. But while I'm not completely present, I'm present enough. I'm ready for him. When his arms come up, I drop my whole body backward, taking him off balance. When we land, I hear a loud whoosh. I deliver another blow to the stomach with my elbow before I roll off him and jump to my feet.

"I think she's good," Julian says from the floor, rubbing a hand over his stomach. I grin down at the fae, pleased with my success.

"Agree to disagree," Derek mumbles. My head jerks up in his direction. The feeling of success evaporates as I narrow my eyes at him.

"Anyone ever tell you positive reinforcement works better than negative?"

"No, actually they haven't." His response is so quick and bitter that it stops me for a moment. I glance at Julian as Derek turns away. The other fae jumps to his feet before giving me a little shrug and leaving. I turn back to Derek, watching the muscles in his back tense under my gaze. He reaches for a cup of water, taking a swig.

Since we left the palace, I feel like Derek has been showing more and more of his true colors. Even going as far as opening up, without actually opening up. Like right now. One sentence, and it tells me so much.

"Let's try something else," I say, because I know he won't take well to me offering any sympathy right now. I'm not supposed to notice his response to my question. That much is true no matter what male I'm talking to. It's a universal character trait.

"Like what?" Derek turns back around, ready to focus on business once again.

"I've been training with Jerome on my water magic. Maybe we can combine the two? I have to learn how to do that eventually."

"I don't think you're ready for that yet. Your magic is still unpredictable, and your fighting skills are basic at best."

"Wow, you sure know how to make a girl swoon," I roll my eyes as he gives me a confused look. Sometimes fae and their honesty is just a little bit too much. But instead of getting offended, I push.

"Maybe so, but I won't learn until you teach me. And you won't teach me until we try it, so it's a vicious circle, and that means we should try it."

"What exactly do you have in mind?" He hasn't agreed, but he's not arguing, so I take that as a good sign.

"I'm thinking Jerome attacks with water, while you attack with a sword, and we'll see if I can keep you both at bay."

"That sounds dangerous."

"Okay, great. Then we're doing it." I don't wait for him to voice any other concerns as I bounce toward the house and yell into the open doorway for Jerome to come outside. He's there a minute later, looking between the two of us.

"What's going on?"

"I need you to attack me with your element, while Derek tries to attack me with a weapon." I announce, grinning.

"Should she look this happy about this? Should you look this happy about this?" Jerome glances between Derek and me.

"Yes, absolutely. I need to know how much I've learned and practice applying it."

When I put it like that, the guys have no reason to argue. Julian and Hannah are now at the back door, watching us curiously, but all my attention is on the guys in front of me. I have absolutely no idea if this will work, but I have to try. The anger I was feeling earlier about the Ancients, and my own lack of progress, fuels me. Granted, I know this isn't how a real battle will go, but I need to know if I can handle the assault from both sides.

Derek picks up his sword, swinging it a couple of times around his body. I glance back at Hannah one more time, but there's no expression on her face. Julian, however, looks a little worried.

The fae don't give me any warning. Suddenly, a wave of water rushes straight out of the ground, sweeping me off my feet. I land hard, but I'm quick to get back up. Derek attacks at the same time, swinging his sword at me. I dodge out of the way, reaching for my magic at the same time.

Another wave comes, but I hold it at bay before grabbing Jerome's water and flinging it at Derek. It slams right into his face, disorienting him enough for me to land a kick. I'm going for the sword, but that doesn't budge. Jerome blasts water at my back, pushing me forward. I'm falling before I can catch myself. I twist around just before I hit the ground, landing on my back. Derek is there, his sword swinging downward. I thrust my hands in front of me, creating a water shield. His sword slams into it and stops.

Happy with myself, I push the whole thing at him as I get to my feet. Jerome sends another water blast at me. I know the moment something goes wrong. My magic shifts, wanting to protect me from the back, slacking on the shield I created at the front. The momentum of Jerome's blast carries me forward instead of back. When I fly through my own water shield, the thing that stops me is Derek's sword.

It rams right into my right arm before either of us can do anything. I scream, dropping to my knees. Derek is instantly beside me.

"I'm—Avery—I'm so sorry." He keeps repeating it over and over, as the pain brings in darkness. I feel myself fading while the fae rush around me. It makes me want to chuckle how human they're acting at this moment. Genuine concern and worry paint their faces.

"Avery, I'm so sorry."

"Wasn't—your—fault," I mumble right before the world goes black.

CHAPTER 12

When I open my eyes, I'm in a bed. It's not the bed in the room Hannah gave me as my own. This one is a little more like what I remember the palace to look like. I turn my head, glancing down at my arm. It's been bandaged from my shoulder to halfway down past my elbow. It's completely stiff, and I can't move it.

"You're awake."

I glance up to find Derek standing at the foot of the bed. At first, I think I'm imagining him, but then he steps toward me and into the light. His face is pale, like a human would look after a bad case of food poisoning. And his face is completely stoic. I realize this must be his room, and that brings a wave of mixed emotions.

"How long was I out?"

"About a day."

That makes me sit up a little farther. Derek is there in a flash to help me sit up. He moves the pillows at my back as I use my left arm to push myself up. His face is only a few inches away, and the desire to touch him almost overwhelms me. Instead, I grip the sheet beneath my fingertip as I settle back against the pillows.

"You cut me. I shouldn't have been out so long."

"I pierced right through your arm with a fae blade. It wouldn't come straight out. We had to...extract it." That means they probably had to cut a bigger hole in me in order to do so. The hesitation in his voice is the only sign of emotion. He's completely shut down. It's much like when I first met him many moons ago in Arizona. Immediately, I miss the fae I've gotten to know since then.

"You could've died."

The words are barely whispered. There he is. He's not meeting my eye now, as if too ashamed to do so. I raise my hand toward him, palm out. Glancing up, he stares at it, as if it's a foreign object, before placing his own in it. I wrap my fingers around his and tug him down on the bed. He sits down carefully, as if he's afraid he's going to hurt me more somehow.

"That wasn't your fault," I say, my words sure and strong. His eyes meet mine. He studies me like he's trying to figure out how much truth is in my statement. I roll my eyes at him, and he furrows his brow in confusion.

"I know I'm not full fae and don't have that whole 'truth only' rule, but I am speaking the truth."

"I should've been able to stop it."

"How? Plus, it wasn't your idea in the first place."

"Exactly." He moves to stand, but I grab onto his arm, keeping him in place. His skin is hot under my touch. He stares at the spot for a moment before looking up again.

"I was bound to get hurt eventually, Derek. I know that's not exactly comforting, but I can't learn if I don't try."

"There has to be another way."

"There isn't. My next lesson with this might very well be an actual fight with actual bad guys and more magic and more weapons. I would be a liability, and I won't be that again."

"You're not."

"But I am." I sigh because even as I'm talking to him, I'm realizing a lot of these things for myself. Maybe I already knew them but saying them out loud is making them more real. "Everything about me is a liability. I can't control my magic, the elemental aspects of it. And now, I can't control the faery magic either. I need to be able to access it and understand it. I can't keep relying on chance, which is what happened in that forest."

"I don't think you give yourself enough credit."

"I think I gave myself too much. Between lessons with Jerome on elemental magic history with Hannah, and you and Julian teaching me fighting, I feel like I don't know anything." I stop, taking a deep breath, because I don't want to cry in front of him.

"My whole life, I prided myself on my education. It's what I did best, learn. Now, I feel like that whole time I've learned nothing. I'm completely blind in this situation, and I have no grounding point to help me find my footing. I can't be babied or protected. I have to do the work."

I'm a little out of breath when I finish my speech, but I'm not sorry. Derek might not understand where I'm coming from, but at least he'll have the information in front of him.

"I don't want to see you hurt."

"It'll hap—"

"No, don't just except this as the outcome. Fight to not make that an option. I need you safe, Avery. I won't be able to live with myself if something happens to you."

His words stun me into silence. It's the most emotion I've ever seen in him. For a second, I have no idea what to do with that. Then, I slide my hand down his arm, taking his hand once again in mine and giving it a small squeeze.

"I know I've failed you," he continues, watching our hands entwined together on top of the covers. "I don't want to be like her, Avery, but sometimes I can't help it." I don't have to ask who he's talking about. I've met his mother. "Spending time in the human world has taught me to be more sympathetic, which is something I was never taught as a child. If the time comes, I might not be able to turn that part of me off. But for you, I want to try."

79

This time, when tears pool in my eyes, I don't hide them from him. He's opening up to me in a way I never imagined. So vulnerable and so human. For the first time, I actually know for a fact there is no manipulation here. He's speaking from his heart, however far away it may be hidden.

Giving his hand another squeeze, I let the tear slip down my cheek before I whisper, "I forgive you."

* * *

IT TAKES me three full days of staying in bed before I can venture out. According to Hannah, I lost too much blood. On top of my already magic-exhausted body, that means it took me longer than it should've to recover. I also wasn't allowed to practice any of the said magic, but Hannah made sure to bring me plenty of books on Faery to keep me occupied.

The more I learn about this land, the more fascinated and sadder I get. It's beautiful, full of traditions and magical stories that I've never even heard of. But it's also full of cruelty and darkness and madness. It breaks my heart knowing that Derek and Julian, and even Hannah, have had to live in this.

I think of my parents and how angry I've been at them for keeping this secret from me. But at the same time, I miss them so much it hurts. After reading more about this place, I'm also thankful to them for not letting me grow up like that. They have always been there for me, they have played with me and taught me rhymes and song. They made sure we had picnics in the park and mushroom hunts in the forest. They were there, and that presence and their love is what I remember most.

Fae don't exactly operate the same way. Many send their offspring off to be raised by servants or tutors, depending on their standing within the courts. Even when they're left at court, they're looked after by nannies. I can't help but think about Derek and what kind of upbringing he had. He clearly doesn't have a good relationship with the queen, and I'm not surprised. She seems like she'd be the worst at being a mother. I won't pry, no matter how much I want to. But one thing I wish I did know is why she only has the one son. Or maybe I'm missing something.

"How are you today?" Hannah steps into the room without knocking. I have moved back into my room. Still unsure why I ended up in Derek's originally.

"I've been moving around fine. I'm ready to do more."

Hannah studies me carefully, as if trying to find the validity in my words. Today, she's wearing a deep green gown with a long cut all the way up her thigh. The spaghetti straps are barely visible as they hold the dress up. She looks effortlessly beautiful. It reminds me that I'm still in my leggings and t-shirt. I don't know why seeing her dressed up always makes me feel so self-conscious, but it does. I really need to get over it.

"If you're sure," she says, her eyes still narrowed on me. I push my shoulders back to try to appear stronger. She doesn't miss the move. "What do you have in mind then?"

"I want to work on the pages."

She knows exactly what I'm talking about of course. We've been putting off me reading anything from the Ancient's book until I was a bit more stable in my magic. But now it seems that time is running out, and we have no choice but to try. We've been gone long enough that I'm getting nervous about Queen Svetlana showing up and dragging me back, kicking and screaming. After lying in bed for three days, I'm not wasting any more time.

"You seem very determined."

"I think it's time. This land needs me, Hannah. I'm not saying I'm going to save everyone. But I want to do my part. I have to."

She stares at me for another long moment, as if waiting for me to back down, but I won't. Whatever it does to me, I have to try.

"Okay," Hannah finally agrees, turning to head back out of the room. "Do we tell the boys?"

"No."

My quick answer makes her pause, turning to glance over her shoulder at me. I'm not backing down from that either. Derek is too protective right now, and Julian isn't far behind. I think Jerome would understand, but it's not like he needs to know. Hannah doesn't comment. She only leads me back to her rooms.

Once inside, she shuts the double doors, waving her hand over the edges. I'm not sure what kind of magic she possesses. She never displays it all, but she's a powerful fae. I'm not surprised she has a few tricks up her sleeve. Walking over to her nightstand, she opens the top drawer and pulls out the two pieces of paper.

Immediately, the magic inside me wakes up, pulling me toward the bed where she leaves them lying. I walk over, glancing at the words without reading them. I haven't truly read the book since the day in the library when I found it.

"So, I just read the spell?"

"It's not really that simple." Hannah walks over to the opposite side of the bed before facing me. "Just like with any powerful magic, you must carry intention in every word. Since these words are transcribed by fae from thousands of years ago, they already carry with them intention. As you read the words, you must over-power the initial intention and make the words your own."

"Like taking ownership."

Hannah smiles. "Exactly like taking ownership."

I glance back down at the pages. From what I remember before I sent these to Hannah at Thunderbird Academy, they contained at least two spells and some history. The book I found was written almost like a journal. It's like someone was telling a story and then filled in the gaps with spells and diagrams and graphs.

"I'm not sure I can do that."

"You won't know until you try."

"That contradicts the whole part where you were telling me to be careful."

"I will give you guidance from both ends of the spectrum,

Avery. You have to be the deciding factor. It's what will fuel your magic."

That makes sense, even though it seems impossible for me to thrust any kind of will on an ancient artifact.

"Okay, I'm ready."

"When you read the words, read them in your mind. They do have to be spoken out loud, in the correct order, which isn't always what is written. That is why you read it in your head first. But don't linger. If something doesn't make sense, keep going. Read the passages as a whole, never individually."

I do have a tendency to get stuck in a word or a sentence and try and figure it out before moving on. Apparently, it's a bad habit. I'll have to keep that in mind.

"Whenever you're ready, Avery."

"Queen Svetlana won't be able to track it?"

"Not here."

I'm going to have to ask more about that later. Right now, I turn to the pages and begin to read.

CHAPTER 13

I don't touch the pages at first. Even though I said I'm ready, the nervous feeling at the pit of my stomach intensifies the closer I get. There really isn't an easy way to do this. I have to stay focused, and I have to dive right in.

Picking up the first page, I flip it over to go to the beginning. There's a drawing of a tree with no leaves in the left corner and some branches at the chapter heading. The number five stands out on its own at the top. Taking another deep, calming breath, I begin to read.

The words don't have to rearrange themselves or jump out at me in any way. They look like any other book I've ever read. And I've read plenty. These pages are a continuation of something I read at Thunderbird Academy, the passage that started it all. Hannah watches silently as I begin to read.

The true knight is not only a person but an idea. There are those who believe the power comes from within, and there are those who believe the power comes from the land itself. It never matters where it comes from, as long as the one who wields it, wields it with a pure heart.

. . .

THE STORIES of brave young magicians have been passed down for generations. And yet, they are not to be found hitherto. Ballads and folk-tales have been created, yet none can truly sing of the grandeur of such a being.

IN THE TIME before time began, they used to say fae came from the heavens above. Angels sent to the land to nourish it and grow it. But the hearts are wicked above all else, and the beautiful creatures lost sight of their mission and became greedy. They created boundaries and warred among themselves, searching for the rush of the ultimate power. They created creatures to serve them as they became their masters, and the land did not grow but withered. Until it could handle no more.

I GLANCE up at Hannah then, as the page comes to another break. She's watching me carefully, waiting for me make my move. The same sadness I felt in the Faery wasteland has entered my heart once more. I didn't think I was still so connected to the land, but maybe that's part of my magic, and it will never go away.

"I don't really understand the pages. Or this book."

"What do you mean?"

"It's written in small paragraphs, and it seems to jump from a journal entry to a bedtime story to actual historical information."

Hannah is silent for a moment, thinking over it.

"When you read it, do you sense the same type of emotions from each passage?"

It's tempting to glance down and read over certain parts, but I restrain myself. Instead, I close my eyes, trying to process what I'm feeling without focusing on the words. It's difficult, since that's not how my mind usually processes information. After a few moments, I shake my head.

VALIA LIND

"No, they don't seem the same. You're saying multiple authors wrote this?"

"It appears to be so. It's not unheard of. Maybe it was a specific family or a specific court that was entrusted with information."

"So, it's not an Ancient who wrote it."

"I can't answer that, Avery." Hannah shrugs, flipping her long hair over her shoulder. "I don't have more knowledge about them than you do. They are a very taboo subject around these parts."

That part I already knew. Seeing no other choice, I take a second to settle my mind once more before I glance down at the paper.

THERE WERE those who believed the land created the true knights to protect herself. Others thought they were angels sent to replace the ones who became the power-hungry fae. Those with the belief of pure creation would fight to protect the land at any cost. It is why those creatures were the most rewarded. Marks were bestowed on the pure hearted, gifts from the land herself. Some hid such marks, and some wore them proudly.

"MARKS?" I mumble out loud, and the moment I do, my focus shifts.

"Avery!" Hannah's voice is raised in alarm, and I release my fingers to drop the page, but it's too late. The words pour out of me as I read them, the need so overpowering, I can't stop.

"The fae with the purest hearts, with the strongest minds, those with the right intentions. They were meant to rule Faery because Faery wanted to be ruled by them. But the greed was too strong and the fae were too weak to overcome the basis of what was asked of them. To let the land thrive and the pure of heart rule—"

Suddenly, the space around me is thrown into a windstorm. I

86

hold onto the page, afraid it'll be ripped away from me as I stand in the midst of a tunnel. Magic surges through me, rushing through every nerve ending on my body. I can feel it everywhere. I close my eyes, leaning into the rush, wanting more of it.

There's a loud banging somewhere close by and shouting, but I don't care. All I want to do is to stay in the cocoon of this wind and in the ecstasy of this power running through me. The high is almost too much and not enough at the same time.

More shouting reaches me. A huge explosion rocks the floor I stand on, but I don't lose focus of the want that fills me.

I want more.

I want more.

I want more.

The shouting comes again, this time closer. I hear my name called over and over.

I know that voice.

Opening my eyes, I turn to the left to find Derek just on the outside of the wind vortex His face is pale and frantic as he calls out to me. I want to tell him there's nothing to fear. That this magic isn't bad. That I can control it. But then my eyes drop to his mouth, and his lips form a word that breaks through the fog of power in my brain.

"Please."

Just as suddenly as it comes, the wind is gone. I fall forward with Derek there to catch me. The electricity is still running over my skin, and a part of me wants to get back into whatever it was. It's Derek's touch that grounds me. I finally drop the paper back onto the bed.

* * *

"WHAT WERE YOU THINKING?" Derek shouts about an hour later as we're all gathered in the library. Hannah insisted on me eating and drinking after my ordeal before she allowed Derek within shouting distance. I am thankful for small favors.

I'm still a bit disoriented, and I have no idea what I did. I'm not even sure if it was my doing or some Ancient curse put on the pages. Apparently, that can be a thing too. I'm learning so much these days.

If Derek didn't burst through that door with whatever magical dynamite he has up his sleeve, I'm not sure what would've happened. That is why I'm giving him a minute to get the frustration out. It's strange to see him this frazzled, but a part of me likes it. I should really keep that part to myself.

"Those pages are dangerous. What if that vortex killed you? Did you even think about that before you started to read some ancient text for your amusement? You don't think! You don't think what this will do to—if anything happens to you—" He runs his hand through his hair, sending it dancing into disarray. In this moment, he looks so much like just a gorgeous guy I know and not a prince of the Spring Court. Part of me wants to reach out and hold him.

I'm keeping that part buried as well.

"You can't keep taking risks like that, not with your life. It's stupid to—"

That does it. I glance up at him from where he's been standing behind a chair, gripping it tightly.

"Are you done?" I interrupt, shocking him into silence. It takes him less than a second to recover.

"No, I'm not done."

He walks around the chair, marching straight for me. The intensity in his eyes makes my head spin as he stops three feet in front of me.

"You keep taking these risks, and you think you're just going to be fine. Because why? You're not invincible, so stop acting like you are!"

"You have no right to tell me who to be, Derek." I get right in his face. I'm not intimidated, and I need him to know that. "You want me to be strong? You want me to learn my magic and be able to protect myself? Then deal with the consequences of that. There is no growth without growing pains, and I won't be talked to like a child because you don't like the outcome of something."

"I don't like seeing you hurt!" He screams the words, and they shake the glass on the windows around us. I've forgotten that we're not alone. Hannah, Julian, and Jerome have been watching our spitting match in silence. I can't even begin to read what's on their faces. It doesn't matter because all of my attention is on the fae in front of me.

"You can't protect me from everything," I whisper, matching his intensity but with the opposite volume. His full attention is on me, so I know he's forgotten about our audience just like I have.

"What if I want to protect you?"

My heart clenches at the simple question, heavy and hurting as it fills with emotion. Maybe that's dramatic, but it feels like I'm full, and that's a feeling I've never experienced before.

"You can't protect me from this," I reply honestly. We both know it's true. I'm on a path neither one of us understands, and there's only one option for us, to move forward. "But you can help me."

He nods at that, his eyes still on mine. It really does feel like the whole world falls away. Everything between us is more intense, more emotional. I have no idea when I decided to let him into my heart, but here we are.

"Not to interrupt this lovely moment." Hannah's voice penetrates our gaze, and we jerk to attention, glancing at her. "But we have company."

She doesn't say anything else. Standing, she walks out of the library with all of us on her heels. Instead of going outside, she heads for her room.

"Hannah?" Julian calls out, but she doesn't stop. We follow her in as she stops in front of her large standing mirror, placing her palm against it. It ripples like water would and then someone steps through it.

"Hello there!" Nora says, giving each of us a smile.

All I do is stare in return.

CHAPTER 14

"You have a portal in your room?" Julian asks. I'm glad someone decided to ask because I'm a little confused too. We went through all of that forbidden forest drama for nothing?

"Only for very special occasions," Hannah replies as she reaches over to give Nora a hug. I didn't even know the two knew each other. I really don't know anything about these fae.

"It's not a happy occasion, I'm afraid. The queen has sent me to fetch you back. As far as she knows, you are still in the forest looking for her elusive book. So, she allowed me the use of portal magic to bring you back. She just didn't know where I was portaling to." Nora shrugs, giving each of us a once over. "Oh hey, Jerome."

"Hey."

I glance between the two fae. I'm sure I'm not the only one who notices the tone in that one greeting. Curious.

"Why are we needed back?" I decide to concentrate on the issue at hand. I'll have to ask Nora about Jerome later.

"I'm not exactly sure, only that it was urgent."

I glance over at Derek and see him deep in thought. There's

something going on, but I can't even begin to guess what it may be.

"How urgent?" he finally asks.

"Urgent enough that we need to leave now."

My only thought is that I'm not ready. I need more time with the pages, I need more time with training. Going back now will be going into the lion's den with no protection. But I also realize I don't have a choice. The internal panic comes anyway. So that's great.

I turn to Hannah, but she beats me to it. "I'll keep them safe. This place is still not on anyone's map." I nod at that. She looks like she's going to say something else, but she moves back away from the mirror instead. Julian and Derek move forward, not even questioning the orders.

"Just like that? We're leaving?"

I'm waiting for the guys to speak up, but they don't. Both of them just look resigned.

"We need to go, Avery, before the queen comes looking herself," Nora urges, holding out her hand to me. I guess we're not even going to grab our stuff or anything. Once again, the choice is taken from me, but this time, at least I expect it. The queen was bound to get restless. Or she decided on a new game.

"If you need us, you know where to find us," Jerome calls out, and I realize this is a goodbye for now. I almost say thank you, but I stop myself, giving them a smile instead. Hannah watches me steadily. I hate that we didn't have time to talk about what happened. I have so many questions.

My skin is still buzzing from the magic, and I'm itching to get back to the book. But there's no way I'm taking the pages with me, and therefore, I'm out of time and out of luck.

The guys step through the portal first and then Nora and I follow. We come out in my room. It feels like I haven't even left, even though it's been over a week now.

I head for the door, but Nora stops me.

"You can't go like that. She'll expect you to look like you've been in a forest for days."

I glance down at my leggings and t-shirt, realizing she's right. I rush into the walk-in closet with Nora right behind me. She pulls a dress out as I tug the shirt over my head. It's a simple flowery dress, barely falling to my knees. The spaghetti straps are a little thicker. When I pull it over my head, I feel like I'm going to a picnic in the park. I tug the leggings off and slip into some flats.

"Well?"

"We'll just say your clothes were too disgusting for her majesty."

"Good plan."

We rush out of the closet where the guys are waiting by the door. Derek gives me a quick once over, his eyes lighting up at the sight of me in this dress. I don't have time to process that because there's a knock on the door. Julian pulls it open to find guards on the other side.

"She is to come with us," the one at the front says, nodding at me. Nora and Derek move to follow, but the guard puts up a hand. "Just her."

We exchange a look, but it's not like we can argue. I give Derek one last look and then I let the guards usher me out of my room and toward the queen.

"Ah, good. You're here. Did you bring it back?" the queen asks the moment we step into the throne room. Her body lounges on the throne like it's a sofa.

"We weren't able to locate it," I reply. The queen doesn't even bother to look disappointed.

"That is truly a shame," she says, and means the complete opposite. Even though I knew this was all a game to her, I'm still mad. She was never going to entrust me with any of her books. And now I'm not even sure she has any. Maybe this was a test to see if I would lead her to the book.

"You have requested my presence urgently. We didn't want to

delay," I reply with my best smile. For a queen who's been in power for generations, I'm sure she sees right through it. At least I tried.

"Yes, the urgent matter." She stops then, as if she realizes something. "What are you wearing?"

"My clothes were not presentable to be seen in." I smooth the skirt down over my thighs. The queen narrows her eyes but doesn't comment further.

"Back to the matter at hand, I'm having a ball, and you are to attend. It's time you met the others within the Spring Court. That is all."

Wait, what? She turns away from me, back to the fae sitting at her feet. I don't even want to know what they were doing before I came in, or will continue to do when I leave. I'm dismissed just like that. The guards usher me out before I can make a sound.

A party? In the middle of a war? That sounds great.

*　*　*

NORA IS in my room when I return.

"A ball? She's throwing a party?" I ask, exasperated the moment the door closes behind me. The queen is definitely keeping a close watch on me. My used-to-be shadows are full-on ghosts now, following me whenever I go.

"I can't really explain that to you either," Nora says, standing near my walk-in closet. She seems excited, so I bite.

"Nora, what's in my closet?"

The fae claps her hands together before motioning to follow her. She does a sweeping motion over what hangs there. I can't believe my eyes.

"Is that?"

"Brand new. Just for you."

"You've outdone yourself." And I mean it. I just can't wrap my mind around the fact that the dress is the exact replica of the one I wore in my time leap in the house.

The color is bright magenta, the shoulders open, with a halter top and a deep v-cut in the front. It stitches at my waist before falling out in a flair skirt to the floor. It's elegant and simple, and so me. You'd think the color clashes with the green streaks in my hair, but it compliments them somehow instead.

"You really like it?" Nora asks. There's a strange catch in her voice. Glancing over at her, I find her watching me carefully.

"Why wouldn't I?"

"I'm not sure. I know it's flashier than you like, but once I got the idea in my head, I couldn't let it go."

It really is a beautiful gown, even though the whole situation seems strange. But then again, is it really that strange? If what I saw in the house was truly the future, or one possibility of it, this dress was bound to come around. I guess maybe I didn't want it to be real because I didn't like the way I felt in that garden with Derek. That feeling is what I remember more than what we were talking about.

"You did a lovely job, Nora." It's the closest to a thank you that I will get with her, but it's enough. She beams at me, satisfied. "Do you know anything about this ball?"

Nora sobers up instantly. I knew something was up with this party besides what's on the surface.

"I can't be sure of anything, Avery."

"But?"

"But there has been talk that the queen has a special announcement to make. All the top families are commanded to be there. The preparations have been going on for a few days now."

"And you have no idea what it could be?"

Nora shakes her head as I try to come up with possibilities. She ended our mission before we managed to get anything done. Granted, she didn't exactly know we weren't looking for the queen's books. Still, if she wanted me to have the books, there's a way for her to get them to me. If she wanted to help, she would.

There has to be some devious plan behind this sudden party. The land around her is turmoil, the Ancients are pressing in at the borders, and she wants to host all the high-ranking families in her court? We have to be ready for the worst type of outcome.

"I'll see what I can find out," Nora comments, and I smile in response. The party is in two days, so I have until then to get ready. I'm not exactly sure what I will do, but it feels like having an exit strategy is my best bet. I wonder what Derek thinks about all of this. We've been separated since the moment we returned.

"I'm going to go ahead and wash up," I announce. Nora hurries to grab fresh towels.

It still surprises me sometimes just how modern this place is. The fae have truly adopted the century the world is residing in, even though time really has no meaning to them. I suppose that's what happens when you live for hundreds of years.

I accept the towels from Nora and head to the bathroom. A part of me is tempted to soak in the gorgeous bath, but that would make me a little too vulnerable for my liking. So, shower it is.

The moment I'm under the warm spray, I let my mind focus on creating a to-do list. If I'm to have a way out, I need some supplies. Maybe Nora can find me another one of those handy over-the-shoulder bags I had to leave behind at Hannah's.

The more I think about leaving, the more I think I need to do that anyway. Being in Spring Court has yielded me no help. Maybe there's a way I can go back to Hannah's. Or better yet, I can get out of Faery all together and find a better place to hide. Although, I'm not exactly sure where that would be. The Ancients seem to be able to find me anywhere.

I suppress the shiver that runs down my spine at the thought of the creatures. The last dream, or vision, that I had with them is still sitting heavily on my mind and heart. No matter how mad I might be at my parents, I want them protected at all cost. And

BLOOD OF THE FAE

that's exactly how far the Ancients are willing to go to get what they want, so it's a no-win situation for me. Unless I can figure something out.

It feels like I'm missing crucial information. Even after reading the page from the fae book, there's so much I don't know. But I do feel more connected to it all. That scares me all in itself. Every single day I think I'm getting closer to losing complete control. I'm a bomb waiting to go off, and someone has already lit the wick.

CHAPTER 15

The next two days go by in a blur of activity. Preparations for the ball continue as if the whole existence of the court depends on the success of it. I can't say that's making me feel any better about anything that's going on.

Derek has been completely missing in action. I saw him once across the courtyard, but he barely just met my eye before disappearing again. I've been training with Julian instead. He's a great sparring partner, but he's no Derek. I try not to let his absence bother me. I have more pressing issues to deal with anyway.

Nora has been great at prepping my to-go pack, if the need arises. I'm not sure when I decided to trust her, but we've become almost like friends. She spends all her time with me, and I know that's partially because she's been assigned to watch me. But there's also an actual friendship forming between us. Just like there is one with Julian.

These fae are so different from anything I've ever imagined, it's hard to reconcile with the image sometimes. I'm still careful, but even so, I've allowed myself to really be present when I'm with them.

"What would you like me to do with your hair?" Nora asks

after I've showered and moisturized. The one thing I do enjoy about fae, to a point, is their vanity. Because of it, I have access to the best oils in the world. Since I have to wear such a revealing dress, I want to make sure my skin glows.

It feels very strange having such vain thoughts if I'm being honest.

"I think down and straight will be fine," I reply, sitting down in front of the vanity mirror as Nora takes her position behind me.

"Are you sure about the no curls?"

"Okay, how about waves?" I ask with a smile. Nora really enjoys this part of her job, and I kind of want to give her the chance to do it. She beams at me before taking the damp strands into her hands. She brushes my hair out before using her hands and magic to dry it and give it a slight wave. I have no desire to wear paint on my face like I've seen other fae do. I'm thankful that wasn't a requirement from the queen. Instead, I just dab on two coats of mascara, accenting my already long lashes, and leave it at that.

Since coming to Faery, and especially after my fae powers began emerging, my features have sharpened in a way. My eyes are brighter, my cheeks carry the glow of an artistically applied highlighter. Even my eyebrows don't need any filling in. They're still my features, but more vivid somehow.

The process of applying mascara still calms me in a way, giving me a sense of normalcy I've been so desperately craving. I'm not even sure where such a human object came from, but I'm happy to hold it in my hands.

"What do you think?" Nora asks. I glance into the mirror to see her smiling at me. My hair is shiny, with a barely-there wave that makes it fall gracefully around my shoulders. The green streak that appeared after I used my fae magic for the first time fits me somehow, mixing with my dark brown hair.

"You did a great job," I say, receiving a quick squeeze on my shoulder from the excitement.

"Come, let's get you into this dress."

I stand, dropping my robe from my shoulders as Nora holds out the dress. In the time that I've spent here, I've definitely become more comfortable in my own skin. I think it's a combination of things. The training has definitely helped me to feel more confident. But it's also just my mindset. So much is placed on my shoulders, but if I don't believe in myself, no one else will. Making a plan and making progress has helped me see that I can handle this. I hold on to that ray of sunshine of a thought as hard as I can.

The material is silky against my skin, and it sends a dance of goosebumps down my arms. The back of the dress is lower than I would like, but it also makes me feel good somehow. Once the dress settles over my hips, I run my hands down the sides, enjoying the feel of it. That's when I realize something awesome.

"I didn't know you added pockets."

"Only on the right side. And it's more of a slit than a pocket. I know you'll want to be armed."

Curious, I watch as Nora walks over to my vanity table and pulls out something from the top drawer. It's looks like a leather belt, but when I look closer, I realize exactly what it is.

"Where did you get that?"

"Derek wanted to make sure you had it."

I pull the dress up and slide the leather band over my upper thigh. It sits there comfortably, and when I slip the knife into the sheath, I feel stronger. The dress falls down over my legs and then I place my hand in my pocket. When I do, I feel the knife there. The opening is perfect for me to reach it if I need it.

"This is incredible."

"Glad you think so."

When I turn and look at myself in the long mirror, I'm surprised by how right I look. It's as if I belong here with my hair falling across my naked shoulders, the knife strapped to my thigh. The fact that Derek wanted to make sure I had it warms my heart, but I don't comment on it. I push that away and focus on the task at hand.

Tonight is going to be a long and interesting night. I can feel it.

* * *

When it's time to head to the main hall where the majority of the festivities will be held, Nora leads me out. Even though I've been preparing for this mentally and physically for days, I'm still nervous. It would be very dumb of me not to be. This allows me to stay on my toes. At least, I hope it does.

My increased focus is why I realize we're not heading toward the hall when we leave my room behind.

"Nora?"

"Trust me, Avery."

Since I haven't had a reason not to before, I don't say anything. But my hand is in my pocket, reaching for the knife just in case. When Nora turns, veering off the main hallway, I realize where we're going. The courtyard opens up in front of us, and it looks much like it did in my vision.

The trees are bigger, and the flowers are in full bloom, sending the whole area into an eerie glow. It's beautiful and a bit frightening all at the same time.

"What am I doing here?" I ask Nora, but she doesn't reply. She just nods her head in the direction of the courtyard, so I have no choice but to leave her behind and walk into the garden.

I feel him before I see him. He's standing near one of the trees at the back of the yard, his dark suit accenting his broad shoulders. He turns, even though I'm sure I haven't made a sound, as if he's sensing me as well.

"Avery."

"Derek."

I stop a few feet in front of him, and honestly, I don't know what to say besides his name. He looks incredibly handsome in his suit, which I now can see is dark blue. The light shirt under-neath is unbuttoned at the throat. It's such a small detail, but it makes it so much more him. His hair is slicked back at the sides, but even so, he doesn't look quite as polished as he might be trying to be.

"You've been avoiding me," I say, deciding on the direct approach.

"It was necessary."

"How so?"

"The queen commanded it. I could not disobey."

There he goes with his formal speech again. It makes him sound so unapproachable, which is probably what he's going for. Except, he's the one who brought me here.

"So, what about now? You're allowed to talk to me?"

"No."

The one-word answer surprises me. I truly did not think he could go against a direct order from the queen. But then I notice the visible strain on him, and that makes sense. He's breaking her command, and it's costing him. I just don't understand why.

"What's going on, Derek?"

He doesn't answer right away, as if he's trying to find the right words. Or trying to push them past his lips. I really have no idea how faery magic affects this whole situation, but it was important enough for him to try, so I wait him out.

"I want you to be ready, Avery," he finally says, taking the slightest step toward me. "Faery revels are—they are not for the faint of heart. I know—" he hurries on to add, as if he realizes what he just implied, "—I know you can handle yourself, but be on the lookout. Don't...don't eat or drink anything unless Nora or Julian hands it to you."

I notice how he doesn't put himself in that category.

"Where will you be?"

"Near the queen. I am to be beside her the whole evening unless she commands otherwise."

The anger I feel toward that fae is finding new heights. I hate how she manipulates everything and everyone around her. The power she holds over her son breaks my heart. Because she uses it to her own benefit. Someone really needs to teach her a lesson. Or better yet, give her a taste of her own medicine.

"Why can't I eat anything? I've been eating faery food for weeks now."

I know the rules for mortals. If a mortal eats faery fruit, they won't want to leave. Ever. They'll be addicted, and most of the time, they become slaves. But faery food doesn't affect me the same, or I would've felt it by now.

"This is different."

"How so?"

"I can't really explain it, but there are a lot of very powerful fae present. They can do things...things that can have consequences. So be careful."

I close my eyes briefly, taking a deep breath. This whole evening was already making me nervous, and now I'm extra nervous. I need to stay calm and collected.

"I'll be watching over you," Derek says before he pushes past me. I think he's gone, but then his voice reaches out to me. "I'll always be watching over you."

So many thoughts rush over me at those whispered words. It doesn't feel like a hastily spoken phrase. It feels like a promise.

A promise a fae prince just made to me.

The quiet of the night is shattered by my emotions. I wish there was a way I could go after him and tell him that I'll be watching over him as well. The connection I feel toward him intensifies anytime he's near me. He's become that to me, and I have no idea what I will do with that information.

But there's just me and the trees. He's gone.

And I am left all alone.

CHAPTER 16

*W*hen Nora and I finally walk into the main hall, it is already filled with fae of every kind. Their clothes are much more elaborate than what I am wearing, but I don't feel out of place. That in itself is very surprising to me. Maybe I'm becoming accustomed to this life. Or maybe I'm still thinking about Derek's words and every little emotion they evoked.

Stay alert.

Stay alert.

Stay alert.

I have to repeat this to myself, because it's way too easy to get lost in a daydream. Now is not the time nor the place. The queen notices me right away. She is seated at the other side of the room in a raised platform. She motions me forward, and I walk across the floor to present myself in front of her throne. Derek is standing right over her right shoulder. It's taking everything in me not to stare at him. I steal a brief glance, but even that isn't missed by Queen Svetlana, so she grins knowingly at me when I stop in front of the throne.

"Welcome, Avery," she says, her voice carrying across the way. Everyone seems to quiet down at once. "You are our honored guest this evening, so I want to start it off with an old tradition." I glance over at Nora, who has moved to stand with the crowd, but she can't help me now. "The first dance."

With those words, the floor at my back clears, as the fae move out of the way and to the sides. I turn, confused as to what exactly is happening when the queen stands.

"The first dance is an old tradition that has not been part of our revels for a while. But tonight, on this special occasion, I would like to ask my son, Prince Derek, to lead our esteemed guest, Avery, in a waltz."

My eyes fly up to meet Derek's immediately. It's only because I've come to know him so well that I see the twinge of shock in his expression before it shuts down. There is no choice here, no way for either of us to say no.

"Go on," The queen urges, and that's when I realize what she's doing. There's a smug smile on her face, and it can only mean one thing. She wants to embarrass me. What teenage girl actually knows how to waltz. Or dance in front of a crowd.

Derek steps down from the platform, offering his arm to me. I have no choice but to take it. He leads me to the middle of the dance floor, sliding his hand down my arm and giving my fingers a quick squeeze.

"Just do the best you can," he murmurs, just loud enough for me to hear. "And don't let them see you sweat."

It's such a human thing to say that I almost smile. Instead, I steel my features, looking up at the prince. He guides one of my hands to his shoulder while he takes the other into his own. When he steps forward and wraps his hand around my waist, I forget to breathe. Our bodies brush just barely. I look up to find his intense gaze on mine.

"Lead the way," I whisper as the music starts.

Derek takes another pause and then he steps forward. My movements are automatic as I trust his leading and fall into rhythm. There's a bit of an audible hush over the crowd, as if they too expected me to stumble.

But one thing the queen or the fae here don't know is that my father taught me how to waltz when I was just a little girl. He continued to dance with me on many occasions. I can see now how it may have been a way to prepare me for this life, if the need ever arose. It's like how those childhood rhymes carried the truth about Faery in them. Our dance lessons were a way to teach me not only self-confidence, but a way to keep myself on the winning side if I ever ended up in court.

When Derek spins me, I see Queen Svetlana's face for the briefest of moments. Her gaze is hard because her plan clearly didn't work. I have no idea why she wants to see me fail in front of all these fae, but she does. Whatever her plan is, I one upped her, and that's going to cost me. I know that for a fact.

But right now, as Derek's hand around my waist pulls me even closer as we spin, I don't want to think about any of that. He moves like someone who is meant to do this with elegance and grace. Even though he's clearly much better at it than I, there is no hesitation in my movements. I think it's simply because I am dancing with *him*.

We have found our footing together, and we glide across the floor as if we've been doing it all of our lives. His skin feels hot under my touch, his shoulders strong and sure under my fingertips. He holds me close but with a gentleness that I have come to expect from him when it comes to me. It's much like when he carried me across the forbidden forest, cradled in his arms.

The whole court falls away as we spin and spin. I think I could dance with him forever, if ever given the chance. It's a dangerous thought and one I shouldn't be having. But as I look into his eyes, I think he might be thinking the exact same thing.

We're a match in every way. Even in this small aspect, even though this dance doesn't feel all that small at all.

It feels more significant than I'd like to admit. I'm not exactly sure what to do with that information.

For now, I let Derek lead me as I hold onto him and forget every terrible thing that has happened to me since I got here.

* * *

WHEN THE MUSIC FINALLY FADES, the court erupts in applause. Derek spins me out, so that I can take a bow, before walking me back over to the queen.

"It seems you are full of surprises," she says, looking down at me. She's unhappy with me. I don't have to be a mind reader to know that. It would be a helpful trait right now because I still have no idea what her intentions are.

"You may go and mingle." The queen looks over at Nora, who hurries over to stand beside me. I incline my head at the queen before I follow Nora to the edge of the room.

"Avery, that was incredible. I didn't know you could dance!" Nora gushes as soon as we're out of earshot of the queen. After that ordeal, I want to slump against the wall and eat some chicken nuggets or something, but I know I have to keep up with appearances. So, I give Nora a quick smile.

"My father was big on educating me in many ways."

"Well, if I ever get to meet him, I'd like to thank him for that myself. The look on her face—"

"Nora." I lower my voice because the last thing I want is for someone to overhear our conversation and get Nora in trouble. But I do give her a bit of a bump with my shoulder, which makes her grin.

"Let's get you something to drink," she says, leading me to one of the tables set up at the edge of the room. Apparently, there will be no official dinner, as this is more of a celebration, which apparently has me as the esteemed guest. But there is food piled on every table, enough to feed these fae, and then some, for days.

I glance over my shoulder. Almost involuntarily, my eyes find Derek. He's back to standing beside the queen as she speaks with a man that has eaten too many donuts in his day. He's shaped like one of them, which is not something I ever thought I'd see in Faery. They have the most perfect complexion, so it looks out of sorts, especially since his face is red and sweaty. I can see the gleam even from over here.

"Who's that?" I ask, nodding at the man.

"Oh, that's one of the human ambassadors. Queen Svetlana has quite a few, and they usually come to these sorts of things."

"A human?" That makes sense then. It's why he seems so dull in color compared to the rest of the people here. I give the crowd another scan, and I realize there are a few humans here. I'm not sure how I feel about that.

"She has been in power for a long time, Avery. There's a reason for that."

Of course. It's smart to make allies, even if they're human ones. I wonder what the man does for a living in the human realm. He has to be someone high up, maybe a politician or a business owner. He looks like he could fit the part.

"Beautiful dancing." Julian appears at my side just as Nora pours me a cup of juice and hands it to me. The fountain that sits in the middle of this table is filled with a pinkish substance, which I assume is faery nectar. It smells sweet and delicious.

"I do have some tricks up my sleeve." I smile at Julian before taking a sip.

"There are no sleeves on your dress, but you do look great in it." He winks, and I roll my eyes at his poor attempt at charm. Sometimes, he really is a lost cause. And at other times, he's as smooth as butter.

"Does that mean you get the next dance?" I ask, which is met by silence. I look up to see Nora and Julian exchange a glance. "What?"

"You're technically not allowed to dance with anyone else. The queen must choose your partner each time."

"Well, that seems strange." Then again, I'm at a revel in Faery while there's a magical war going on. Oh, and I have wings. Everything is strange right now.

"She told me to go mingle. What does that entail?" I ask, taking another sip.

"Just make a circle, be seen," Julian replies. "And keep Nora near you at all times."

Before I can question that any further, someone calls his name, and he's gone. I give the room a thorough study, amazed at just how many fae are here. I guess I should say individual bodies, since not only fae are present. But I'm not actually supposed to talk to any of them? I think I can handle that just fine.

"Let's walk," I say. So, Nora and I do.

It's another hour before the queen calls me to her side. The noise level has truly gone up in the room, fae and humans alike having a little bit too much to drink. There's dancing and groping and a lot of laughter. Nora and I try to stay as much out of the way as possible, but there's really nowhere to go.

When the queen summons me, I'm almost glad. Maybe I can finally know what all of this is about.

"Derek, be a dear, and come stand beside Avery."

The moment queen begins talking, every eye is turned to her.

"Now, my fellow courtesans, I have the best news to share with you all." Derek comes to stand beside me and shifts to be a bit closer at her words. I can feel the tension in him, just like it's in me. I have a feeling I'm not going to like whatever she has to say.

"You are all aware of the awful assault our borders have received in the last year. Faery is holding strong, as we all know she will, but there are steps to be taken to see that she succeeds." She glances over at me before continuing with a smile. "A great power has been given to us, a witch with the Ancient's tongue on her lips. And she is here to help us."

She's spinning a story, trying to show her subjects her strength without giving away too much information. I make my face clean of all emotion as I watch her give her speech.

"This great power needs a home, and I am so pleased to announce that now, it will have one."

The confusion that I feel at that is coupled with dread and rightfully so. Because Queen Svetlana's next words shatter my world.

"May I present to you, Prince Derek and Princess Avery, for they are bound for marriage from here on to the end of times."

CHAPTER 17

There's a hush over the crowd, as if they're waiting for the queen to say she's joking. I'm waiting for her to say that she's joking. Whatever I expected, it wasn't this. It was never this.

Don't panic.

Don't panic.

Don't panic.

I learned about fae betrothals briefly when I was with Hannah. It was in one of the history books. Once an announcement is made, it cannot be unmade. But an announcement by the queen herself? It carries extra weight.

Keeping my expression as neutral as possible, I glance up at Derek. He's completely still, not even his eyes are blinking. What I wouldn't give to know what's going on in that head of his. It's taking all of my self-control not to panic. Not to visibly freak out.

I have to stay calm.

I have to stay calm.

I have to stay calm.

I'm about to be yelling at myself non-stop. What is happening?

When applause erupts this time, I visibly jump, making queen's smile broader. She lets the claps die down, and I know she's relishing in this. No one in this court is happy about this. I can see that by their stares. If the power she's talking about is truly present in me, she just announced to the whole court that she will have control over it.

Because just like she can control Derek with her magic, if Derek and I are married, she gets control of mine.

Don't cry.

Don't cry.

Don't cry.

Angry tears. Sad tears. It doesn't matter. I want to scream. I want to set this whole place on fire. I want to drown Queen Svetlana in one of those faery fountains she loves so much. The panic is turning to rage. I can feel my magic building. My hand is tingling, as if it's ready to set the fire and water at the court.

I feel a slight pressure on my hand when Derek's fingers wrap around it. He gives me a gentle squeeze. It's his only outward reaction to what the queen just announced. I hold onto his hand like it's my lifeline. There's no way he knew about this. No way.

"Let us celebrate!" Queen Svetlana's voice booms out across the crowd. The music starts playing again, and her guests have no choice but to act joyous. Everything is falling apart. I can't seem to find the will to move.

The queen steps down from the podium, coming to stand in front of us.

"Do you like my surprise, Avery?" she asks, grinning. There's so much smugness in that expression. I would like nothing more than to wipe it off with my fist. Derek gives me another squeeze, as if he can tell what I'm thinking.

"You really think Derek and I will be married?" I ask, even though I know the answer. I'm really hoping I remembered the information wrong, but of course, that's not the case.

"You will be. Sooner rather than later. We need to get that

power of yours under control and then we need to do some good with it."

"You won't get away with this," I reply, shaking my head. There is no way I will succumb to her control. There must be something I can do. I will figure it out. I promise it right here and right now.

"Oh, but I will. You should have been smarter, Avery. I have been around a long time. I know all the tricks in the book."

Except she doesn't. No matter how powerful she is, she can't read the ancient books. That's why she needs me. That thought will fuel whatever I have to do to get out of it. And I won't fail.

A blast comes unexpectedly, and it's louder than anything I've ever heard before. One moment, there's laughter and shouting in glee, the next, bodies are flying through the air.

I'm thrown backward, losing my grip on Derek as I slam against a wall. Falling forward, I land on my stomach, stunned. Shaking my head, I try to get my bearings, but everything is in chaos. Fae are screaming, there's debris all over the place, and more falling from the holes blown in the walls.

I get to my feet, pushing the hair out of my face as I search for Derek and Nora, who were the closest to me. The queen is in front of me. A sudden urge to end her rises in me. My hand lights up with a fireball. She sees me a moment before I throw it at her. It catches her on her shoulder. The queen screams, her face full of rage.

Another fireball forms in my hand, but before I can throw it, her guards are there, pulling her to safety. Angry at my missed chance, I snuff out the flame as I look for the others.

I find Nora first. She's to my right, covered by another body. There's blood everywhere.

"Nora!" I fall to my knees beside her, afraid of what I'll find. But then she grunts, and I push the body off her as I reach to help her up. "Are you hurt?"

"No." She shakes her head, running her hands over her body. "What was that?"

"I think that was a bomb."

I glance up at the voice, and the relief I feel is almost tangible. Derek pulls me and then Nora to our feet, giving us a quick once-over. His jacket is gone. His shirt is bloodied, but he also seems to be in one piece.

"Have you seen Julian?" I ask, trying to see past the dust settling over the room. I have to shout to be heard over the screams. Then another blast comes, sending us off our feet.

"We need to get out," Derek says, grabbing my hand and dragging me behind him.

"Not without Julian!"

He stops and groans at me, but I'm not about to leave without our friend. Glancing back at the chaos, I try to see if he's anywhere in sight. But there's too much smoke and dust, and too many bodies.

"Avery, we have to go," Nora urges, right as a group of soldiers I've never seen before rushes into the room through the blown-out walls. "We'll find him. But we can't help him if you're caught."

I glance at her, as this all makes sense. They're here for me. The queen paraded me around the court for weeks, and then tonight, provided them a perfect opportunity to come for me.

"Come on!" Nora rushes to the back. I let Derek pull me with him just as the screams become too much to handle.

* * *

THE CHAOS ISN'T CONFINED to the main hall. There are soldiers fighting everywhere. The palace seems to be overrun. Derek keeps a strong hold on my arm as Nora leads the way. Suddenly, he drops my hand as one of the soldiers jumps on him. Another one grabs me around my waist as I scream. My hands ignite with fire, and I grab onto the arms of my attacker. He screams, dropping me. I twist my body around, slamming my blazing hands into his chest. His chest explodes, a hole burned right through him. Horrified, I step back, glancing at my hands and the amount of power I just displayed.

I don't have time to process. Nora's screams reach my ears, and I turn to see her trying to fight off two soldiers. Without hesitation, I send a blast of fire at them, burning them where they stand. Suddenly, Derek is beside me once more, reaching for my hand. He clearly saw what I did, but he doesn't notice. He just pulls me behind him.

We're almost down the hall when I hear it.

"Stop!" I yell. I turn to see Julian rush at one of the soldiers, his sword in hand. The man meets Julian's attack blow by blow. I watch as he begins to gain an advantage.

"Avery—"

I don't wait to hear what Derek is going to say. The fire ignites again, pushing our hands apart but without burning him. Then I'm racing for Julian. On the move, I call on my magic, blasting it straight at the soldier. The man doesn't see it coming. The fire sweeps him off his feet, dropping him ten feet away. Julian follows the solider with his eyes before turning to me in surprise. The surprise quickly turns into relief and then he's running toward me.

One of the soldiers is suddenly there, grabbing for me. I don't hesitate to slam my elbow into his stomach before dropping my weight and throwing him over my shoulder. Jumping to my feet, I blast a stream of fire straight down, burning through the man. When I look up, I see Derek and Julian completely shocked as they look at what I just did.

"What? I had good teachers." I grin and send another fire blast at the soldiers coming for us. The boys seem to snap out of it and then Derek is reaching for me once more. We take off down the hall, dodging fights as much as possible. When we round the corner, Nora is pressed against the wall. She looks happy the moment she sees us.

"This way," she calls as we reach her before she dives into one of the open doorways. We're right on her heels, and the guys push the doors closed the moment we're inside.

"What are we doing? Can we portal?" I look at Nora, but she's already shaking her head.

"Portal magic is blocked. We have to do this the old-fashioned way." She walks over to a tapestry, pulling it aside. Placing her palm against the wall, she mumbles something I don't quite hear and then the wall moves.

"Secret passages?"

"Absolutely. We hit all the classics." She grins. We move as one, rushing for the passageway and away from the sound of the battle. Derek's hand finds my own again, as if he can't be apart from me for longer than a few seconds. I hold onto him with all I have because I need the comfort too. Everything just spun out of control on us, and we seem to be each other's anchor. Nora presents me with a torch, and I use my fire magic to light it.

"How did they get in?" Julian asks once we're farther down the tunnel, leaving the sounds of battle behind.

"It was planned and executed with perfection. There had to be an inside man," Derek muses out loud. "Someone who knew about the revel, who knew exactly who was the center of attention."

"She played us, Derek," I say, looking up into his handsome face. There's a hard look in his eyes, but it softens when he looks at me.

"She did, but I won't—" He doesn't quite finish that sentence, because right now, we both know he doesn't have a choice. But we'll find a way. We'll figure this out.

"You think it was all about Avery?" Nora asks, and we turn our attention to her.

"Absolutely." Derek doesn't hesitate. "They were looking for something when they arrived, of that I am sure. She's the biggest prize they can find here."

"So, what do we do?" I pull the skirt of my dress a little higher, keeping it from dragging or tripping me. "Can we go back to my room to grab supplies?"

"No, it's too dangerous. There's no direct path to your room from here. Our best bet is the village."

"The servant's village?"

"Yes."

I think back to the last time I was down there, the screams I heard that night. It was the night my wings made their first appearance, and everything changed.

"Who do you think those soldiers work for?" I ask.

"It could be any court," Derek replies slowly, as if he too is mulling over that fact. "The clothes the soldiers wore didn't have any court insignia on them. It was a smart move."

"So, we have no idea who's responsible."

"It doesn't matter who's responsible. Right now, we just need to get you out of here. That's priority number one."

We fall silent after that. The only sound is the distant shouts and the slap of the stone beneath my feet. I shiver at the images those screams evoke, but I don't slow down and I don't stop. There's an urgency to their movements, and Derek's grip on my hand is tight.

This group is determined to protect me, but I'm as determined to protect them as well.

CHAPTER 18

$\mathcal{W}$hen the passageway slopes upward, we pause. The sounds of the battle seemed to have faded, but we really don't know what awaits us once we step out of this tunnel.

"Nora, do you have any idea where this passageway ends?" I ask, because she seems to be the only one with any knowledge of these in the first place.

"The forest? Maybe? I have only very basic information about the tunnels. My mother shared them with me." I've never heard Nora talk about her mother before, and her tone makes me want to ask a hundred questions. Just not right now.

"It should be right on the outskirts of the village, at least if the distance we walked is to be believed," Derek says. All three of us turn to look at him. He doesn't comment further, only shrugs.

When we finally come to a dead end, Nora once again places her palm against the stone and mumbles a few words.

"How is she doing that?" I whisper.

"It's part of her portal keeper magic," Derek whispers back. That makes sense. I truly do forget that Nora, or any of the fae, has any active magic. They don't use it very often at all.

The stone moves with minimal sound, which makes me feel

slightly better. We come out into the night air slowly, but there's not sudden ambush that awaits us. We are in the woods, and now that we're out, I can hear the screaming and the fighting once again. The sound really carries in these woods.

"Come on, we need to move."

We race off after Derek without a second thought. He weaves in and out of the trees. I'm glad I've been training so much because I wouldn't have been able to handle all this running before now. When we reach the edge of the forest, Derek pauses. The village is surprisingly quiet.

"We can't just walk in there like nothing is happening. If the attacker is smart, there will be soldiers waiting to ambush anyone who escaped the palace," Julian says, studying the houses in front of us.

"So, what do we do? They'll probably be checking the forest soon as well," I comment. Julian's head swivels toward me like he hasn't thought of that. We all wait on Derek to make the decision because I sure don't know what to do.

"We have to brave it. We'll go fast, and we'll go quiet. If we can make it into one of the houses, maybe we can buy us some time."

"Derek—"

"We don't have a choice, Avery." He glances down at me before giving my hand a reassuring squeeze. "Like you said, the forest isn't safe either, and we have to go past the village to get out. It's our only choice."

I don't like it, but he's right. It's not like we can go back. And from what I know about magic, the tunnels are probably not safe either. If they have a way to suppress portal magic, they have a way to track magic. That means, the tunnels might be discovered. We can't take that risk.

"Let's go individually."

"No, we'll go in twos."

I'm not a fan, but I don't have time to argue as Derek pulls me after him. We move together, keeping pace with each other as if we've been doing this forever. It's kind of like the dance. I can anticipate his moves, and he can anticipate mine.

We reach the first building with no problems, and we flatten ourselves against it the best we can. Glancing behind, I see Nora and Julian rush toward us. I hold my breath until they're beside me. It's difficult not to make any noise, considering everything here seems to be standing still. After another moment, Derek guides me to the next building and then the next. It's like we're playing hide and seek, except we have no idea how many people are looking for us.

Just when I think no one is actually at the village, a group of soldiers comes around the corner. Derek and I drop down behind a barrel, and I really hope luck is on our side. I'm not exactly inconspicuous in my bright dress. Neither is Nora in her green one, although hers is a little better.

The soldiers call out to each other in hushed tones, and I realize they're probably going house to house now. A movement catches my attention. I glance over to the house on my left to see the shades move to the side and then a pair of small eyes finds mine. There's a bit of movement and the child gets yanked away from the window, but after a moment, an older pair of eyes replaces the tiny slit. At the sight of us, they grow bigger and then the shades move over more so that I can see the face.

It's the woman whose child I saved last time I was at the village.

She knows exactly who I am. When she motions for us, I don't hesitate. Derek pulls me down when I stand, but I just shake my head, asking him to trust me with my eyes. Thankfully, that's all it takes because he allows me to pull him behind me. We round the corner just as the door at the back of the house opens, and we rush in. The door closes, but I stop the woman.

"My friends," I whisper, and then Julian and Nora are there. The woman shuts the door behind them, bolting it in place. We all crouch close to the floor, afraid to cast any unnecessary shadows around the house. I glance over to see the little boy peeking from around a table. His eyes on me, and I smile. After a second, he smiles back.

"They're looking for you, miss," the woman whispers, getting down to her knees beside us. "You as well, your highness. I heard them shouting before they went quiet. But they didn't leave."

"Is there a way to get out of here without being seen?" I ask, but the woman is already shaking her head.

"They have the road covered, miss. And magic is blocked."

"So, there's nothing we can do?" I glance at Derek, and he's already shaking his head. He's worried, that much I can see. I am too.

"You can stay here till the morning, miss," the woman continues. I really shouldn't be surprised she's talking to me and not Derek. The gratefulness on her face is evident, and I give her a warm smile.

"If you get caught—"

"Oh, but we won't, miss. Here." She motions for us to follow, and we move quickly across the floor to the opposite side of the kitchen. The woman moves a few bags of grain over and then pulls the rug up.

"We have a cellar."

THE CELLAR IS dark and cooler than the temperature outside, but it's big enough to fit all four of us, and for that I am grateful. The woman waits until we find our places on the ground before she shuts the door and places the rug back over it, cutting off most of the light. A few slivers of light sneak in through the wooden floor, but it's not enough to dissipate the darkness. Nora and Julian are leaning against the wall on my right. Derek and I are sitting right near the ladder. I shiver a little. I'm not sure if it's the adrenaline leaving or if it's the dampness.

"May I?" Derek's words are whispered into my ear. I turn to find his face barely inches from mine. In the near darkness, I still manage to see him somehow, but I don't know what he's asking.

"What?"

"You're shivering. May we share body heat?"

It's such a strange way to ask that I nearly chuckle. But he's serious, and after a moment's hesitation say yes.

He scoots even closer before I feel his arm come around me, and I lean against his broad chest. The feeling of security envelopes me just as his body heat warms me up. I fit against him as if I'm made to be there, and I finally let my mind wander.

I'm betrothed to him. Somehow, someway, I ended up betrothed to the prince of the Spring Court. I have no idea how I'm supposed to feel about that. True, Derek and I—we aren't enemies anymore. At least, not entirely. My feelings toward him have changed. I can't deny that.

But marrying him under the queen's command? It's the worst thing that can happen to me. Not because of him, but because of her. That's surprising all on its own. If this happened even a few months ago, I'd be completely against the idea. But being married to him wouldn't be so bad, I suppose. Except for the part where the queen would control my magic.

I won't allow that.

I won't allow that.

I won't allow that.

"We'll find a way out," Derek whispers against my hair. It's like he knows what I'm thinking about. Maybe he's thinking about it too. I want to ask him about it, but maybe I'm a coward because I don't. I don't know if I want to know his exact thoughts on the situation.

A chorus of voices snaps us to attention. The next thing we know, there's a sound of a door banging open and boots stomping into the house. A deep male voice asks something in a language I don't understand, and the woman answers. There are more questions and more answers as someone continues to walk around the house.

I don't dare to breathe too loudly as we all wait to see what happens. The strange language throws me off a bit, and I make a mental note to ask about it later. It seems like forever, but then finally, the voices and the stomping fades before disappearing entirely.

Yet, still, no one moves, and no one speaks. We're not about to take any chances. And so, we sit like that, in intense silence, until the sun finally comes up.

When the woman pulls back the rug and opens the hatch, I feel like it's been days. I blink at the sudden light before untangling myself from Derek. Neither one of us slept, but he held me tightly all through the night.

"The soldiers have moved down into the forest, miss. Now is your chance."

We rush for the surface. I stop near the woman, reaching to give her shoulder a squeeze. The words 'thank you' are on my tongue, but I stop them before I can utter them. That will never be safe here.

"You have done us a great service," I say instead. She beams at me like I've given her the moon.

"It's the least I could do, miss," she replies, as her little boy pokes his head out from behind his mother's skirt. I give them both a big smile before I join my friends at the door.

"We have to move fast," Derek says, and I shrug.

"What else is new?"

We open the door, and after a quick look around, we run. The houses are still quiet, and the soldiers are nowhere to be seen, but we do the best we can to stay quiet and fast. When the forest is in sight, I almost sigh in relief. But then, I nearly stumble back when I see who steps out of the shadows, right at the edge of the trees.

"Avery, come on."

Derek drags me behind him as we reach Hannah.

"What are you doing here?" I can't help but ask. The other fae rolls her eyes.

"Nice to see you too, Avery. Lovely dress you got on there," she comments. "If you must know, I was looking for you."

"So, you came to the edge of the village forest?"

Even though I don't want to be suspicious, the thought of an insider being behind this attack is at the front of my mind. I definitely don't want Hannah to be the bad guy here, but the coincidence is too much.

"Not quite."

"Hannah."

"Look, don't make a big deal of it, but I spelled you in case I needed to find you. It was a one-time thing."

"What?" I almost forget that we're in hiding as I stare at the fae in front of me.

"It came in handy." She shrugs.

"You people are unbelievable." I throw my hands up in the air, pulling away from Derek. This is all too much, and I'm way too tired.

"Look, don't get all twisted up. I heard of the attack. I came to help. A thanks would be appreciated."

This earns her a roll of the eyes from me, but she isn't deterred.

"You have one shot, darling." She looks at Derek, apparently done dealing with me for the moment. "Where to?"

Derek is silent for a moment, glancing over at me before replying.

"Human realm."

"We're going back?" I immediately forget my grumpiness and walk over to Derek.

"It's the safest bet right now. I need to get you out of Faery."

"But how? Portal magic has been suppressed."

"Only for those within the vicinity. Oh honey, don't look so shocked. I do have some magic up my sleeve," she says, winking at me. "But we better hurry. I don't like being out in the open like this."

Derek doesn't hesitate, giving Hannah a go-ahead nod. Julian and Nora don't offer their opinion. They both look as exhausted as I feel.

"Good luck. To all of you," Hannah says, but her eyes are entirely on me. She waves her hand in the air, saying a few words. Then the space ripples, and I see familiar pine trees on the other side. "Off you go."

Nora and Julian step through first and then Derek takes my hand and pulls me through with him. I turn back around as Hannah raises her hand to close the portal. Something catches her attention off to the side. In the next moment, soldiers are there. They grab her by the arms as one slaps her across the face.

"Hannah!" I yell, ready to jump back through the portal. Derek's arms close around my middle, catching me and keeping me in place. I watch helplessly as Hannah is pushed to her knees. One of the soldiers grabs her face in his hand. There's a look of pure defiance on her face before she spits in his face. The solider backhands her, and she falls out of the grip of the others.

She glances up, her eyes meeting mine through the portal before she yells and swings her arm down. The portal disappears, taking the image of Hannah with it.

CHAPTER 19

I slump against Derek for a moment before I twist in his arms and slap at his chest.

"I could've helped her!" I yell, completely aware of how emotionally I'm reacting and not caring in the least. Hannah has become important to me. And I feel guilty. I suspected her there for a moment. Maybe that moment is what cost her her freedom, if not her life.

"We couldn't have helped her."

"I could've tried."

"Avery. Avery!" Derek doesn't raise a hand to defend himself. He just takes my smacks, giving me a moment to feel my emotions. I know it's not his fault, not really. So I stop, dropping my forehead against his chest. Breathing heavily, I try to rein in everything I'm feeling. The rational part of me knows I'm exhausted and emotional. But I also feel helpless about the whole situation, and I'm so tired of feeling this way.

"Come on, we need to get going."

"Can they track us?" I ask. Derek gives my waist a quick squeeze before stepping back.

"No. They can't track Hannah's portals, but we shouldn't take the risk."

I nod, turning to go. Julian and Nora have been standing quietly, waiting for me to stop my tantrum. Nora reaches for me, entwining her arm through the crook of my elbow and pulling me close. We offer each other what support we can as we follow Derek down the road.

Hannah opened up a portal right at the edge of the human woods, so it's easy to follow the road. Cars pass us by, but we're far enough from the highway that no one offers us a ride. It's probably better that way. When a gas station comes into sight, I breathe a sigh of relief.

We wait on the side of the road as Julian goes inside to grab us water and information.

"We're in Arizona. Near Flagstaff," he announces, handing over bottles of water. I'm assuming he glamoured the clerk into handing those over, since we have no cash on us. His words surprise me, but Derek seems to expect them.

"We need a car," Derek comments and then walks off toward the parking lot. I'm not even going to comment on what he's about to do because all I want is to be back to the cabin. I assume that's where we're going. The Ancients may have found us there before, but I'm really hoping Derek has a plan for that. I need to get out of this dress, and I need time alone to deal with everything that's happened. This was an exhausting twenty-four hours to say the least.

When a dark green SUV pulls up beside us, I'm not even surprised. We pile in, with me in the passenger seat next to Derek, while Nora and Julian get in the back.

We don't speak the whole way there, as if each of us is lost in our own thoughts. Maybe I should be thinking over everything, but my mind is completely shut down. If I let myself think about it, I'll lose it all over again. I can't do that in front of them. Not again.

To say that I'm embarrassed I did in the first place is an under-statement.

No one wants to follow a leader that can't keep their crap together. And that's the level I'm at right now. I think if Derek wasn't here taking care of things, I would've just laid down in the woods and gone to sleep.

Okay, now I'm just being dramatic, and I need to stop.

When we pull up to the cabin, it takes me a second to realize we arrived. Julian and Nora get out first, both heading for the house to give it a check, I'm sure. Derek stays in the driver's seat for a moment, as if waiting me out. I glance over, finding his eyes on me. Somehow, I know what he's thinking.

The last time we were here, things changed between us. Now, things are different again. I have no idea what to do with those thoughts, so I push the door open and get out.

"Welcome back," Derek comments over my shoulder. I don't turn around as I walk into the house.

* * *

I RACE for the shower because I know it's the only place I can be alone. Also, I want to wash all the grime off me. The water feels heavenly against my skin. Even though my water magic wants to come out to play, I don't let it. This cabin is our sanctuary for now. Even though the magic is protected and can't be traced, I'm paranoid.

Every time I think that everything is okay, it all goes up in flames.

When tears leak out of my eyes and mingle with the water from the shower, it doesn't even register that I'm crying. I don't even know what I'm crying about. It just seems like the only thing that can release this pressure I'm feeling. So, I let it.

I am entirely different person than I was when I first came here, and even that Avery wasn't who I thought. It seems that my life is spinning out of control, and I'm just trying to hold on to something before I get thrown off the ride. I let the frustration and the exhaustion bubble for so long, and now I'm finally letting it free. Questions press on me from every side. I'm not getting any closer to answers. So far, all that's happened has made my situation worse. Now, I have to figure out how to fix it.

Once I feel like I can face the group without losing my cool, I turn the water off and get out. Since we left without packing last time, my clothes are still here. I pull on dark leggings as well as an oversized sweatshirt, and I leave my hair down.

When I make it downstairs, Nora and Julian are on the couch. Derek is in the kitchen. The next moment, he comes out, carrying two steaming mugs in his hands, handing one to me. I notice Nora and Julian have mugs in their hands already.

"Green tea?" I ask. Derek nods with a small smile. When I settle on the couch, we each take a sip, none of us sure what to say next.

"So, this has been an interesting revel," Julian finally says. For some reason, I find that funny. The laugh bubbles inside of me, and I don't suppress it. Soon, we're all laughing. In this one moment, everything does seem like it'll be okay. But the feeling doesn't last because that's not our reality right now.

"What do we do now?" Nora asks, voicing the one question on our minds.

"We rest," Derek replies. "And we regroup."

"Do you think Queen Svetlana is alive?"

"She's alive." Derek doesn't hesitate to reply. I wonder if he'd know if she wasn't. "I'm sure she'll have control over her court soon enough and then she'll be coming after us."

By *us* he of course means him, me, and the betrothal she sprung on us.

"How long?"

"There's no way to know. But we'll do what we can. It'll be okay."

"I'm glad you're so optimistic," I reply, not bothering to hide my emotions. "All of this? It's one big freaking mess. Now I'm being hunted by other courts on top of the Ancients? That sounds just swell."

The bitterness in my voice is evident, but I don't care. Apparently, my emotions are coming in waves. So, I'm just riding them at this point.

"We'll figure it out. You know we will. It's the exhaustion speaking. We all need rest."

He's right, of course, not that I'll admit it. I just feel all over right now. The shower didn't seem to help as much as I would've liked it to.

"Are we taking guard duty?" I ask as I stand. I'm ready to rest, but I will do my part as well.

"No. We'll rest. This place is safe."

I take that at face value as I head back up the stairs and toward my old room. I really hope I can turn my mind off long enough to rest.

CHAPTER 20

*T*ossing and turning, I try to find a comfortable position. No matter what I do, I just can't relax enough to sleep. After trying for a few hours, I finally get out of bed and tiptoe downstairs. The cabin is completely still. The rest of the group clearly didn't have the same hiccups I do.

I can't tell where all this pent-up energy is coming from. I'm not sure why my emotions are so unbalanced. I've always worked hard at keeping everything under control. Now I can't seem to keep any of it where it needs to be.

Stepping outside onto the porch, I breathe in the fresh air. I really love this place, even though I probably won't admit it to Derek. The magically created lake opens up in front of me. I feel called to it.

When I reach the edge, I step right into the water, moving my feet around to create little waves. Being near water does wonders to calm me, and I almost let my magic roam free. But not yet.

The space around me darkens suddenly. I spin around, looking for the source. When my eyes land on the creature, I'm not even surprised. He floats a few feet off the ground, his robes moving in the gentle breeze.

"You are back. We knew you would return."

"That just makes you slightly logical. I wouldn't pat myself on the back yet." The words escape me, bitterness dripping off each syllable. This is partially their fault. They could've left me alone. If they did, I never would've gone to Faery in the first place.

"You are growing surer, Avery Kincaid."

I stop whatever retort I had on my tongue as I try to remember if the creature has ever called me by my full name. I honestly can't remember.

"I am growing tireder," I reply, because it's true. I should be treading carefully here, but that doesn't seem to be my response right now.

"You will bring the book to us."

"Why do you want it so much? Don't you already know what's written in there?"

The question seems to honestly baffle the creature because he doesn't respond right away. I can almost see him thinking it through.

"We have been around a long time, young one. Our magic is strong, but our memory is not as long. Centuries have gone by while we slept."

I'm surprised I'm getting any of this information. It's like the creature wants to talk about it. Maybe he was the one who wrote the journal entries in the book I read. Those passages seemed so... human. Maybe that's what the creature is so desperate to reclaim.

"You have read the book."

It's not a question, but I answer anyway. There's doesn't seem to be any reason not to. "Only a few pages."

"The magic is on you."

"On me?"

"We are growing impatient, Avery Kincaid." The tone of voice changes suddenly, as if a switch has turned on. My heart grows cold at the sound, and now I'm back to being afraid. "The book. Bring us the book."

"You no longer want my help to get into Faery?"

"You are there no longer so we have no use for you there. The book is your concern now."

"And if I don't?"

"We have said it once, and we will say it again, we will do whatever it takes." The creature pauses for a moment, as if giving me a chance to prepare myself for its next words. "Your parents are well, Avery Kincaid. They won't be for much longer."

"No!" The word escapes me as the creature begins to fade.

"They will be the first, and then, everyone you hold dear will follow, starting with your fae prince."

"You can't!"

"It is already done."

My heart drops while the horror of that statement fills me. I fall to my knees as the creature disappears and the space around me grows lighter. It's difficult to breathe, but I force air into my lungs.

Derek.

Derek.

My prince.

I gulp air down, concentrating on doing the motions.

My parents are in danger.

My parents are in danger.

My parents are in danger.

I can't seem to think past that statement. I can't seem to stop spinning.

I can't—

I can't—

I can't—

"Avery?" Derek is suddenly in front of me, dropping to his knees in the sand. One look at my face and he stands, spinning around to make sure there is no present danger. Satisfied, he drops back down. This time, he reaches for me. I don't even hesitate.

Falling into his open arms, I cling to him as the air returns to my lungs. I'm a rational individual. I can come up with a plan, and I can execute it. I will not give in to my panic. I will not.

"What happened? Avery?"

"I'm fine. Everything is fine. I think I just had a panic attack, that's all."

"I felt it."

That makes me pull back as I look up into his face.

"You felt it?"

"Yes, I—" He stops, furrowing his brow in confusion. He's not used to this, and I can't blame him. The connection between us has only grown with time. Now, it seems to be at another level. Neither one of us understands it, that much I can tell. But we've become something I never imagined. If this was another time and place, maybe we could explore that further.

I know what I have to do, and Derek will never forgive me for it. None of them will. But I can't let my parents die, I just can't. And I have to protect Derek. And the rest of them. It doesn't matter how I feel about Derek or how he may feel about me.

I guess it's just not meant to be.

He's still trying to figure out what to say when I reach over and place my hand on his cheek. He freezes immediately, his eyes flying over to meet mine. I give him a small smile, rubbing my thumb over his smooth skin. The fae really are so beautiful, but he's even more so. No matter how much everyone tries to make him be a certain type of a prince, he's one with his own mind. And his mind is just as beautiful.

He's going to be so mad.

He probably won't want anything to do with me.

Maybe right here and now is all we will ever have.

So, I do something that I've been wanting do for ages. I close the distance between us, and I catch his lips in a kiss. There's no hesitation on his part.

He's just as hungry for me as I am for him. His arms wrap around my torso, pulling me to him. We both get to our knees while our lips devour each other. He tastes like the most beautiful sunrise and the most relaxing bath. He's all the good things and all the perfect little things, and in this one moment, I give myself completely over to him.

If I could, I would bottle this feeling up and carry it against my heart for an eternity. And then, it still wouldn't be long enough.

When I pull back, I place my forehead against his as we both breathe heavily.

"Avery," he whispers. I put my finger over his mouth because I can't listen to anything he has to say. Instead, I close my eyes, a tear slipping free as I place my other hand at the back of his neck. My lips move but no sound comes and then he slumps against me, completely knocked out.

Placing a soft kiss to his temple, I move him to the ground putting him on his back. Sometimes I forget that I'm a witch above all else. A sleeping spell might not be my best weapon, but it is one I learned a long time ago.

Making sure he's comfortable on the ground, I give him one last look before I jump to my feet and race toward the cabin. The keys to the car are on the counter where Derek had left them.

I put on my shoes, grab a bottle of water and then I'm out the front door.

When he wakes up, he's going to be furious. Nora and Julian will be too. But I have to see my parents, and I have to find a way to protect not only them, but the fae as well.

I was better on my own.

I was less distracted.

I was stronger.

I keep repeating the phrases to myself, willing them to be true. As I drive back into the city, I realize I'm only lying to myself. Yet, it doesn't matter.

I will do whatever it takes to protect those I love. Even if that means doing it all alone.

NOTE FROM THE AUTHOR

Thank you for reading my book! If you have enjoyed it, please consider leaving a review. Reviews are like gold to authors and are a huge help!

They help authors get more visibility, and help readers make a decision!

And, if you'd like to know what's coming next, sign up for my newsletter today!

CLICK HERE TO SIGN UP!

Thank you!

NEXT IN THE FAE CHRONICLES SERIES

Preorder today: Revenge of the Fae

After the bloodshed we left behind in Faery, my magic is more desired than ever.

But my one concern is saving my parents. Even if it means leaving the fae prince behind.

I will stop at nothing to protect those I love. Even if it costs me my life.

Featuring a fierce heroine, a broody prince, and all things magical, Revenge of the Fae is the explosive conclusion to this fast-paced young adult paranormal romance series from the USA Today bestselling author Valia Lind!

Click here to preorder today!

DO YOU LIKE ACADEMY ADVENTURE ROMANCE?

Get the complete series here:
Thunderbird Academy Trilogy

My power could save my friends—or destroy them.

As I start a new semester at Thunderbird Academy, I have a lot to live up to. News of my sisters' courageous fight against the Ancient evil has spread, and now, everyone expects the same greatness from me.

But all I want to do is:
  1) Find my dad.
  2) Figure out why my magic has suddenly gone on the fritz.

It would be a lot easier if I didn't have to keep dealing with the ever-annoying Aiden Lawson. Shifter, nemesis, ridiculously gorgeous. I don't care how he makes my pulse race, I will not be deterred from my mission.

But the war with the Ancients is just beginning, and now, Thunderbird Academy has become a sanctuary as well as a school. Each attack is deadlier than the last, and when the academy ends up under siege, my friends and I have no choice but to fight.

Am I brave enough to trust my magic to save us? Or will my world come crashing down around me by my own hands?

I'm in a fight for my life, and I, Maddie Hawthorne, have no idea what I'm doing.

Welcome to my year at Thunderbird Academy.

Full of magic, adventure, and romance, Thunderbird Academy is an completed addicting young adult paranormal romance series by USA Today bestselling author Valia Lind that will keep you reading late into the night!

WANT MORE FROM THE HAWTHORNE WITCHES?

See Harper and Brianna, Maddie's sisters, take on the Ancients in the complete season one of Hawthorne Chronicles!

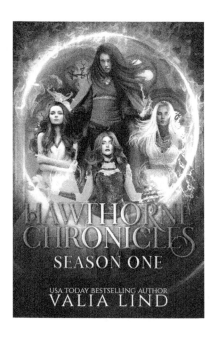

Charmed meets The Originals in this exciting paranormal romance series by USA Today bestselling author Valia Lind!

Welcome to Hawthorne. A town. A home. A sanctuary.

It's a land of magic, where traditions run deep. Governed by an ancient coven, it's a place where supernaturals and humans can live in peace.

Until now.

An Ancient evil is rising on the outskirts of their town and it's up to the Hawthorne coven to find a way to defeat it or their way of life is over.

Four strong witches. Four incredible romances. Four life or death battles.

Can one town stand against an Ancient evil?

Season One includes:

Guardian Witch

Witch's Fire

Witch's Heart

Tempest Witch

Get hooked on witches, shifters, and magic in this first season of a thrilling adventure!

ABOUT THE AUTHOR

USA Today bestselling author. Photographer. Artist. Born and raised in St. Petersburg, Russia, Valia Lind has always had a love for the written word. She wrote her first published book on the bathroom floor of her dormitory, while procrastinating to study for her college classes. Upon graduation, she has moved her writing to more respectable places, and has found her voice in Young Adult fiction. Her YA thriller, Pieces of Revenge is the recipient of the 2015 Moonbeam Children's Book Award.

Sign up to receive a newsletter for new releases and sales!
- https://bit.ly/2Ovd3fX

ALSO BY VALIA LIND

Hawthorne Chronicles - Each season can be read as standalone!

Season Three

Marked by Fae (prequel novella) - free to download

Shadow of the Fae (#1)

Blood of the Fae (#2)

Revenge of the Fae (#3) - Coming Summer 2021!

Season Two

Of Water and Moonlight (Thunderbird Academy, #1)

Of Destiny and Illusions (Thunderbird Academy, #2)

Of Storms and Triumphs (Thunderbird Academy, #3)

Season One

Guardian Witch (Hawthorne Chronicles, #1)

Witch's Fire (Hawthorne Chronicles, #2)

Witch's Heart (Hawthorne Chronicles, #3)

Tempest Witch (Hawthorne Chronicles, #4)

The Complete Season One Box Set

Crooked Windows Inn Cozy Mysteries

Once Upon a Witch #1

Two Can Witch the Game #2 - coming Spring 2021!

Blackwood Supernatural Prison Series

Witch Condemned (#1)

Witch Unchained (#2)

Witch Awakened (#3)

Witch Ascendant (#4) - Coming Summer 2021!

The Skazka Chronicles

Remembering Majyk (The Skazka Chronicles, #1)

Majyk Reborn (The Skazka Chronicles, #2)

The Faithful Soldier (The Skazka Chronicles, #2.5)

Majyk Reclaimed (The Skazka Chronicles, #3)

Havenwood Falls (PNR standalone)

Predestined

The Titanium Trilogy

Pieces of Revenge (Titanium, #1)

Scarred by Vengeance (Titanium, #2)

Ruined in Retribution (Titanium, #3)

Complete Box Set

Falling Duology

Falling by Design

Edge of Falling

Printed in Great Britain
by Amazon

65618389R00088